"Sean Ellis delivers another high-octane romp, exploring mythical lost civilizations and alternative histories, with the unrelenting pace of your favorite summer blockbuster."
Stel Pavlou, bestselling author of *Decipher*

"Sean Ellis never fails to deliver and his latest thriller has everything I look for in a book: monsters, guns, sex appeal and a touch of the supernatural. Mayhem and action abound in this page-turning adventure."
Jeremy Robinson, author of *Instinct* **and** *Threshold*

I0457514

PRAISE FOR SEAN ELLIS

"Sean Ellis delivers again with a globetrotting adventure replete with ancient mysteries, deadly enemies, and creatures out of legend. Ascendant is a thrill ride you'll never forget!"
David Wood, author of *Atlantis*

"Quickly builds up steam into an action packed thrill ride full of mystery, adventure, and a touch of the paranormal. Sean Ellis has written a story that will keep you reading until the wee hours."
Rick Nichols, author of *Survivor's Affair* and *The Affairs of Men*

"Sean Ellis successfully blends the action-adventure of Clive Cussler with the paranormal flair of Dean Koontz—a unique and exciting combination that serves this high octane mystery well."
Rick Chesler, author of *Wired Kingdom* and *kiDNApped*

"Sean Ellis writes action scenes that rival those of Clive Cussler and James Rollins."
James Reasoner, author of *Dust Devils* and *Texas Wind*

"Sean Ellis is a magician, doing it all with a deftness that pulls you in and draws you along from page one breathlessly to the end of the book, offering mysteries galore, bad guys with the blackest hearts and a good old fashioned hero to kick their evil arses."
Steven Savile, author of *Silver*

THE DEVIL YOU KNOW

A NICK KISMET ADVENTURE

SEAN ELLIS

Gryphonwood

Gryphonwood Press

THE DEVIL YOU KNOW. Copyright 2015 by Sean Ellis

Published by Gryphonwood Press.
www.gryphonwoodpress.com

ISBN-10: 1940095271
ISBN-13: 978-1-940095-27-1

BOOKS BY SEAN ELLIS

PROLOGUE

She looked, at that moment, *more lovely than he remembered, and it occurred to him that if her face should be the last sight his eyes beheld, then he would die a lucky man. Then dark spots swam in front of his eyes, eclipsing her beauty and underscoring the simple fact that, lucky or not, he was about to die.*

His gaze swung back to the other face--the shadowed, barely glimpsed visage of his assailant--and he redoubled his efforts to break free. He clawed at the fingers which were clamped vise-like around his neck and which had already dammed the flow of life-sustaining blood to his brain. The fingers were thin, with gnarled knuckles like the branches of a willow tree, and gave no impression of inherent power, yet no amount of prying could loosen the killing grip. He changed tactics, directing his ever-waning strength into punches and kicks, but the dark garments of his assailant seemed to absorb the energy as if he were fighting his own shadow. Panic quickly gained a foothold and his actions, though already ineffectual, became increasingly frantic and all the more futile.

A final rational impulse prompted him to go limp, sagging in his captor's grip as if unconsciousness or death had at last claimed him. But his bluff was as useless as his struggle; the fingers did not relax their grip, even for the measure of a heartbeat. The black spots grew together, completely occluding his vision, and the capitulation of his flesh was no longer an act. Even the noise of his struggle grew indistinct, lost behind a haze of white static that gradually resolved into a sound like the ringing of a....

1

...telephone.

Nick Kismet gazed in faint surprise at the white plastic receiver on his desktop, as if the mere fact of its presence might explain this unexpected interruption. The phone trilled again insistently, but offered no further enlightenment.

He did not get many telephone calls on the office line. Almost everyone who might possibly want to contact him knew his cellular number; in fact, the office number didn't even appear on his business card.

Business card. Who would have ever imagined that? The thought brought a rare smile to his lips, cracking a normally intense, almost brooding expression. A tall man with broad shoulders and an athletic build, Kismet's few acquaintances knew him to be reserved, some would even say anti-social. His dark hair was clipped short, as it had been nearly two decades before when he had begun serving as an ROTC cadet. While his military career had stalled and ultimately transformed into something entirely more individualized in nature, his sense of discipline had never been fully retired.

As the phone commenced another cycle of electronic chirps, he relented and lifted the handset to his ear. "Global Heritage Commission, Nick Kismet speaking."

"Did you get my message?" The voice was feminine, faintly muffled as if the person speaking was attempting to disguise her identity by wrapping a handkerchief around the mouthpiece.

"What mess--" He broke off when the irritating blare of the dial tone began screaming into his ear.

When he spoke again, it was solely for his own consideration. "Well, that was useful."

He almost put the matter out of his mind. It was late, already six in the evening, and while he had never really kept any sort of traditional schedule, there was certainly no reason for him to be in his office in the lowest level of the American Museum of Natural History at this hour. Whoever had made the mysterious call had been lucky to actually reach him; by all rights he should have been en route to his Brooklyn Heights brownstone residence, if not absent from the United States altogether on some far-flung assignment. That the caller hadn't seen fit to actually say anything relevant was barely a cause for concern.

Probably a wrong number.

He logged off his computer and rose to his feet, intent on leaving behind the cryptic communiqué along with all other matters relating to his position as American liaison to the Global Heritage Commission of the United Nations Education, Science, and Cultural Organization. But as he reached for the door handle, his gaze fell upon an object protruding from his threshold. With a perturbed frown, he knelt to pick it up.

It was a glossy tri-fold pamphlet of the kind often found in hotel lobbies touting various tourist destinations. The cover bore the unmistakable outline of the tallest building in New York City. He drew back his hand to toss it away.

What message?

For a moment he did not move; only stared at the paper in his hand, replaying the abrupt monologue of the female caller. At length, he unfolded the tract and was not at all surprised to find written on the shiny paper, in what looked like red grease pencil, a series of numbers: "8:00."

"Eight o'clock at the Empire State Building," he murmured, shaking his head. "You'll have to do better than that."

He then folded back the remaining leaf to expose yet more writing--letters this time--and as the single word written there penetrated his conscious mind, Kismet would have sworn his heart skipped a beat.

Prometheus!

It took every ounce of self-control he could muster for Kismet to refrain from urging the taxi driver to go faster. There was no particular need to rush. He would be arriving at his destination well ahead of the implicit deadline, but he could barely contain his eagerness.

At some level, he regarded the assignation with suspicion. In almost twenty years of searching he had not heard so much as a whisper about the mysterious secret society named for the Titan of Greek mythology. His only knowledge of that group--if indeed it was an organized body--stemmed from a violent encounter with an assassin who had spared his life after massacring an entire family. Yet it was neither that horrific incident nor the unexpected stay of execution that had made the search for the Prometheus group his purpose in life, but rather the strange parting message of the killer:

Kismet, if I killed you, your mother would have my head.

A foundling, Kismet had no idea who his mother was, nor any clue concerning her involvement with the murderers associated with Prometheus.

He gazed at the pamphlet again, examining the scrawled letters in the glow of passing street lamps. Further experimentation, in tandem with his knowledge of the gender of his mysterious contact, had led to the conclusion that the 'ink' was actually a bright crimson shade of lipstick. This revelation did not however relieve him of his anxiety regarding the approaching meeting. There was still every reason to believe that he was walking into a trap.

His singular experience with Prometheus had been deadly and there was no way of knowing if the moratorium on his own death sentence had expired. He had always been circumspect in his search and to the best of his knowledge only a handful of people living, most of them members of the US military, sworn to secrecy, knew of the incident and Kismet's interest in the secret society. Of course, that didn't include the members of Prometheus itself, and therein lay the reason for Kismet's apprehension. Then again, if they wanted him dead, they could have accomplished that goal at any time, and without heralding their intentions.

He gave the cab driver a twenty-dollar bill and hastened toward the Thirty-fourth street entrance. As he passed into the lobby however, he slowed, studying the faces of its occupants for some sign of recognition. Most were obviously tourists; adventurous young couples making a nighttime sojourn to one of the city's most famous landmarks. No one offered more than a cursory glance. He kept walking. Although the message had not indicated a specific place within the massive edifice for the rendezvous, Kismet felt an inexorable pull in defiance of gravity.

As he stepped from the high-speed express elevator, surrounded by people who were easily distinguishable as visitors to the Big Apple rather than residents, it occurred to him that he had never before made this vertical journey. In the descending twilight, the skyline of New York City, as seen from the windswept, open-air observatory on the eighty-sixth floor of the Empire State Building, was an awe-inspiring sight. Despite the urgency of his purpose, Kismet flowed with the human current toward the iron bars that lined the edge of the observation deck and let his eyes rove over the cityscape. Only then did he turn away to see if anyone in the crowd found him more interesting than the view.

Two people immediately caught his attention. They were not standing together but curiously enough seemed to have the same tailor. Both were burly men, looking like nightclub bouncers in sport coats and conspicuous in their choice of semi-formal clothing in such a casual environment. Kismet self-consciously realized that he too looked rather out of place in his charcoal gray two-piece suit. Despite their incongruous appearance, neither of the men were doing anything particularly suspicious. Their eyes periodically wandered from the skyline to glance at the crowd but their curious appraisal fell short of scrutiny.

After a few minutes the tide of spectators began to ebb and most of the tourists lined up to catch the next elevator down. When Kismet looked again, he found that the two men had moved, changed position, but were still there, still making unobtrusive surveys of the group.

They're not interested in me. Who are they watching?

He looked more closely, following their line of sight to determine what the men were really doing. When he finally spied her, Kismet wondered why he hadn't noticed the woman earlier. Like the two watchers, her choice of attire was at odds with the standard uniform of most visitors to the landmark edifice but that was by no means her most noteworthy attribute. A shapely form in a maroon Armani suit, with glistening black ringlets that would have stretched down to the middle of her back if not for the constant winds that buffeted the eighty-sixth floor, she stood peering through one of the coin-operated stationary binoculars positioned at intervals along the edge of the observation area. Below the hem of her dark, mid-thigh length skirt, her sculpted legs were clad in matching fishnet stockings that eventually disappeared into pumps with impossibly thin leather bands and three-inch stiletto heels. Yet it wasn't until she straightened, then turned to look in his direction, that Kismet knew he was looking at the author of the anonymous invitation.

With a wry smile he walked toward her. "I hope you won't think this too forward, miss, but that's an extraordinary shade of lipstick you're wearing."

Up close, the woman who introduced herself as Capri Martelli, was no less a feast for the eyes. Kismet found himself regretting the circumstances that had brought them together; now that the meeting had commenced, he would have to maintain a wary posture.

"You chose an interesting place for this little meeting," he commented after halting pleasantries were exchanged. "Very melodramatic. As was your invitation."

If she took offense at the veiled jab, Capri gave no indication. "Given the sensitivity of the subject at hand, I thought a clandestine approach was called for. I hope I didn't inconvenience you."

"Not yet." He smiled humorlessly and waited for her to make the first move. The silence that followed was almost uncomfortable, but Kismet did not relent.

Her crimson smile finally faltered and she pursed

her lips briefly before speaking again. "I know you must eager to hear what I have to say about Prometheus."

He shrugged. "Like I said, your invitation was hard to resist. I'll reserve judgment on everything else."

"Where should I start?"

She's fishing. "Maybe you should start by telling me who you really are."

"I told you my name, Mr. Kismet. But I don't think that's what you meant. The truth is, I'm a journalist." She grimaced, as if the admission was a source of shame.

Sure you are. Kismet thought about the two men now unobtrusively observing them from a distance. "And why did you contact me?"

"I thought that was obvious. Prometheus."

He folded his arms and leaned against the upright bars, which bordered the perimeter. "Pretend I don't know what that means."

For the first time, her eyes betrayed her. The surprise evident in her expression confirmed that she had expected a very different progression of events. After another awkward silence, Kismet decided to put her out of her misery. "Let me tell you what I think. You heard somebody mention my name and something called 'Prometheus' in the same sentence and thought I'd be eager to tell all. That's not going to happen, Capri."

His decision to use her first name was methodical; it would either put her at ease, as with a familiar, or elevate his status in her eyes to that of an authority figure, a parent or teacher. It was an old interrogator's trick; a skill he had first learned in Army Intelligence. He wasn't completely sure of his stated conclusions but knew that the accusation would force her hand. To reinforce his position, he pushed away from the barrier and began walking toward the elevator lobby.

"Wait!"

The panic in her voice told Kismet he had won. He paused but did not turn to face her. "I'm listening."

She hastened to stand in front of him, and kept her voice low. "I got a tip…an anonymous tip…that said you knew something about Prometheus. I was warned to be very discreet."

"This is your idea of discreet?"

"I didn't think I should just walk into you office. And the phones could be tapped."

He waved his hand in a dismissive gesture. "So you don't really know anything about this… this Prometheus, whatever that is?"

"I know a little." Her eyes darted past him, then swept suspiciously around the observation deck. "Enough to know that Prometheus makes the Illuminati sound like the Boy Scouts."

"A secret society?" Kismet affected skepticism. "Conspiracy theories? What news service did you say you work for?"

"I didn't, Mr. Kismet. I'm employed at the *Clarion*—"

He stiffened apprehensively. The *Clarion* was a daily tabloid, owned by a media mega-corporations, that catered to the lowest of lowbrow readers with sensational stories, lurid photographs and inflammatory editorials. Reporters for the *Clarion* were often accused of impersonating journalists.

Capri cringed at his obvious reaction. "This isn't for the paper. I'm doing a… a research project on secret fraternities. It's a family matter."

Something about the way she had used the word led him to believe that Capri's 'family' was more than just her close blood relatives. He glanced involuntarily at the two suited men; they had changed positions again but remained at a distance, still futilely attempting to blend in with the diminishing crowd. Kismet felt a chill creep over his back that had nothing to do with the relentless wind. A connection between the mysterious group he sought and organized crime was something he had never considered.

"Okay. So how did that lead you to this Prometheus? I've heard about some of these secret societies, but I've never seen a Prometheus mentioned anywhere." It wasn't a lie. More than a decade of searching libraries and archived documents had not yielded a single mention of the organization.

She looked around, as if expecting to find someone eavesdropping, then reached out to take his arm. He did not resist as she guided him back to the perimeter of the observatory and turned him so that they were both facing out into the night. The sky had darkened considerably in stark contrast to the illuminated forest of skyscrapers all around. Three distinct dots of light--helicopters--were moving in a tight formation out over the East River. Kismet almost commented on this, but a moment later Capri surreptitiously pressed something into his hands. It was a cell phone. "Listen to it," she implored.

When he put it to his ear, a mechanical voice was repeating: "To hear your saved message, press 'one' now." He did.

The words that next issued from the tiny speaker sounded even more robotic, electronically distorted to mask the identity of the speaker. "I know about the book you're writing; secret societies and such. But there's one you don't know about. No one knows about it. Prometheus, the oldest of them all. Ask Nick

Kismet at the Global Heritage Commission. He'll tell you all about it. But be careful so no one knows what you're up to."

Kismet frowned as the terse message ended and at a prompt from the automated system, he played it again. Despite the altered modulation, there was something familiar about the speaker's idiom. Yet, it was the content of the message that he found most troubling.

"That's all I've got," said Capri in a low voice. "Listen, I've done research on dozens of groups: the Bavarian Illuminati, the Freemasons, the Carbonari, even the Hong Kong triads. On a fundamental level, they're carbon copies. In a way, they're like locks. Each one has its own identity, a key if you will, usually manifest in a complex arrangement of rituals. But what if there is a master key? A society that spawned all the others and can still control them: Prometheus. Am I right?"

Kismet stared off into the distance. His eyes saw that the strange formation of helicopters was closer, much closer, but his thoughts were elsewhere. *Whoever made that message has the answers. He's got to be on the inside; it's the only explanation. But why use Capri as an intermediary?*

"It's a good theory." He handed the phone back. "I'm sorry, but your informant was wrong. I don't know anything about it."

Though it pained him to do so, he turned his back to her once more and moved toward the exit. Her voice--imploring him to wait, accusing him of falsehood--followed after, but she did not move to physically prevent his departure as before. Perhaps she sensed that this time he would not be swayed.

Part of him wanted to tell her; to trust, or perhaps burden, her with the knowledge he had carried for so long. His considerations weren't solely motivated by the fact that she was very attractive--there might have been a very good reason why the anonymous message had been channeled through a journalist with an interest in secret societies--but he couldn't deny that it was a compelling factor. Ultimately however, he decided not to dance to the tune called by the unknown piper. If the informant wanted to make contact, he obviously knew where to call.

A squeal jarred Kismet from his thoughts. Before his eyes could make sense of the sudden mayhem, moving like a wave across the observation deck, another of his senses detected a clue that instantly alerted him to danger. It was an odor he had not smelled since leaving the military: the acrid fumes of a smoke grenade.

He whirled, flexing his knees like a linebacker preparing to meet a rush, and was immediately caught in the onslaught of panicked tourists stampeding toward the elevator lobby. As he struggled to stand his ground, he could see three separate yellow plumes positioned decisively throughout the area. The fierce wind instantly snatched them away, scattering the smoke before it could form a thick covering cloud, but the hissing pyrotechnic canisters had been more than sufficient to trigger pandemonium.

"Capri!"

As he pushed against the human tide, he could see the two men in suits similarly struggling to reach her position. He still didn't know whether to count them as friend or foe, but their pained expressions gave evidence that they were not the instigators of the minor riot. Kismet didn't believe in coincidences. Whoever had done this was either after him or Capri, or both, and the common thread was Prometheus.

The two watchers had almost reached her when abruptly they were intercepted. Four figures--young men with dark complexions--broke from the outer edge of the horde and formed a ring around Capri. The group looked ridiculous in baggy jeans and t-shirts bearing familiar slogans, but underneath those innocuous trappings, they were tough as nails. The suited pair immediately assumed bellicose stances, but the quartet around Capri appeared unimpressed.

It was over in an instant. The two burly men, relying on their superior size and strength, plunged headlong into the fray only to be overwhelmed by a lightning quick defense. The four young men employed a combination of martial arts and basic street-fighting techniques to put the suited pair on the ground, stunned or unconscious, in the time it took Kismet to break through the crowd.

From the moment the smoke grenades had ignited chaos on the observation deck, Capri had stood motionless near the place where Kismet had first seen her. But the approach of the watchers and the subsequent combat had produced an expression of shocked familiarity. She knew the two men, recognized them on sight, but had not expected them to be here, at the site of her covert meeting with Kismet. When they went down under a flurry of punches and kicks, her mask changed to one of horror. That was all Kismet needed to know.

Two of the young men abruptly turned and seized Capri, each grasping an arm and lifting her off her feet. A third brought out a small syringe and quickly pressed it to her upper arm. Capri struggled against her captors, but it was clear that the contents of the hypodermic were having a soporific effect.

"Let her go!"

The four men regarded Kismet with fierce countenances, but showed no special recognition. To them, he was nothing more than a meddlesome bystander, rushing to the rescue of a damsel in distress. The two holding Capri continued to do so, while their comrades closed with Kismet, eager to dispatch him as they had the earlier pair.

Remembering the failure of Capri's would-be protectors, Kismet feinted toward the nearest attacker then pulled back as the young man committed to a counter-assault in the form of a roundhouse kick aimed at the space where he expected his foe's head to be. Kismet caught the man's foot out of the air and whipped his opponent around, slamming him face first into the iron barrier. Even as the bloodied attacker tumbled unconscious to the deck, Kismet ducked under the fists of a second assailant and launched into the man's mid-section with an old-fashioned football tackle that drove him back into his other companions. Capri slumped to the deck as one of her captors was caught in the collision and the other simply abandoned her in order to join the fight.

Kismet rolled away from the tangle of limbs and squared off against the remaining faux-tourist. The young man tried to retreat, but his back was already against the barrier. Kismet edged closer and raised his fists warily. Although he outweighed the youth by a good twenty points, he did not succumb to overconfidence; the four young men were clearly trained in ground fighting techniques, the same techniques he had learned in the army. But while size wasn't always the determining factor in a close quarters battle, if the combatants were of equal skill, it might make all the difference. He moved in.

The olive-skinned youth threw the first punch.

Kismet made no attempt to block or dodge, but instead tightened the muscles of his abdomen and simply grunted as the blow struck home. Before his attacker could recover, Kismet clapped his hands against the man's head, stunning him with a minimum of effort, and then rammed a knee into his midriff. The youth threw a wild swing that glanced off Kismet's temple and for a moment Kismet saw stars but another knee to the gut left the assailant breathless in a fetal curl on the deck.

Kismet was still seeing double, but he could approximate Capri's location. As he took an unsteady step in her direction however, everything changed. His senses were abruptly assaulted by a deep bass rhythm, a noise that rang in his ears and resonated in his chest cavity. Suddenly, three distinct shapes rose up beyond the limits of the barrier, blasting the deck with the artificial tempest that could only be caused by the rotor wash of a helicopter.

Faster than the eye could follow, three Bell Jet Rangers rose above the level of the barrier and hung in the air, their noses point toward the aerial tower that sprouted from the stout base of the eighty-sixth floor to give the skyscraper its legendary and one-time record breaking altitude. The choppers moved closer, their rotor blades invisibly carving the air dangerously close to the tower. The pilots were hotdoggers; only someone with the skills of an expert and the ego of a daredevil would attempt what they were now doing. It would take only a sudden crosswind to nudge the choppers into the aerial, shattering their rotor vanes and unleashing an unimaginable catastrophe on the unprotected occupants of the observation deck and countless more oblivious souls on the street below.

Spotlights stabbed down from the helicopters,

blinding the onlookers, and ropes unspooled from the side doors to dangle at arm's length from the outside of the palisade. It was as close as the pilots dared get. As soon as the thick lines were deployed, a pair of dark-clad figures quickly abseiled down until they were level with the top of the iron barrier. The metal bars, which rose high above the heads of visitors to the observatory, were bent inward at a forty-five degree angle and ended in sharp points to discourage jumpers. The two men fast-roping from the helicopters had little difficulty pulling themselves over to perch atop the barrier, where they brandished stubby machine pistols. One of them spied Kismet and brought his firearm around intently.

Kismet spun away from Capri's supine form, seeking cover in the huddle of terrified onlookers. A short burst escaped from the automatic weapon and a scattering of rounds chewed up the area where he had been standing, but the airborne commando did not direct his fire into the innocent crowd; it was enough that Kismet had been driven away. A moment later, that same man dropped down onto the deck.

The gunman moved toward the dazed quartet that had first attacked Capri, and began rousing them. The implication was all too clear; the helicopters and their deadly passengers were working in tandem with the youths who had been impersonating tourists. As the men regained their senses, another object descended from the center helicopter and was guided down into the observation area by the man atop the palisade.

Kismet instantly recognized the aluminum-framed wire contraption—search and rescue teams called it a 'Stokes basket'--and just as quickly divined its purpose. In a matter of seconds, the men bundled Capri into the mesh stretcher and secured her with heavy nylon straps. At a signal from the ground force, the litter was drawn back up into the aircraft.

With the gunmen providing cover, the four ersatz tourists moved to the ropes that still dangled from the helicopters on either side and were draped over the spiked barrier. Although only two commandos had rappelled down, a total of six heavy-duty lines had been thrown out, doubtless to facilitate the team's extraction. The men tore off their slogan t-shirts to reveal climbing harnesses outfitted with Jumar ascenders which they hastily secured to the ropes.

On a rational level, Kismet was overwhelmed by the complexity of the two-pronged assault. It was unthinkable that Capri's abductors might have had advanced knowledge of her intention to visit the skyscraper. That meant the operation had been conceived on the fly and executed by a highly trained and well-financed paramilitary team. Kismet knew from experience that the even the famed US Army Delta Force couldn't--or rather wouldn't--attempt such an outrageous undertaking; their unparalleled training notwithstanding, Delta force operators were still limited by political and logistical considerations. He knew of only one group that might be gutsy enough to pull off such an exploit.

But what on earth could Prometheus want with Capri, that would justify such a profligate expenditure of effort and resources?

With the help of the ascender devices, the four men scurried up the ropes and into the middle and right hand copters. Kismet felt his bile rise as the remaining members of the team, still clipped to their ropes, started working their way back up. He could feel adrenaline coursing through his veins, impelling him to take action, but there was nothing he could do to stop them. The ease with which the commandos had carried out their audacious mission felt like a contemptuous slap and all he could do was clench his fists as he cowered with the rest of the frightened tourists.

I don't think so.

He was moving before he knew why, and certainly before he knew what he was going to do. The gunmen noticed him right away, but were too focused on the task at hand to shoot at him; besides, what could he hope to accomplish? As soon as the second man was clear of the palisade, the pilot of the Jet Ranger eased away from the danger zone, pulling the heavy ropes away from the observatory. The other helicopters had already moved back, but were remaining on station until the last two members of the team were aboard. Kismet made a desperate and ultimately futile grab for one of the ropes as it slipped through the bars and dangled free in the night a thousand feet above the street.

He stood there, the sound of his own heartbeat roaring in his ears louder than the thumping rotor blades, and stared at the retreating ropes. They remained tantalizingly close, swaying gently as the commandos ratcheted the cam-locks higher, one step at a time.

"Close enough," he muttered.

The adrenaline gave him just the boost he needed. With near superhuman alacrity, he scrambled up the bars and swung his leg high enough to hook a foot between the needlepoints atop the barrier. The sharp tips snagged his suit jacket, but the wool fabric prevented them from piercing his flesh as he hauled himself onto the angled barricade. He crouched there; his fingers tightly gripping the bars as he flexed his legs like coiled springs, and gathered his courage. His gaze was locked on the quivering rope but he could not completely ignore seductive lure of the void. The emptiness yawned below him, so much air, and below that pinpoints of light marked the movement of motor vehicles on the streets of Manhattan.

Are you gonna do this?

With the endorphin surge momentarily sublimating his most basic primal fear, Nick Kismet drew in a deep breath and jumped off the Empire State Building.

2

In the instant of time it took for him to traverse from building to rope, the helicopter moved, increasing the distance by half again as much. There was a moment of panic as gravity asserted its overwhelming superiority and snatched him down, then abruptly the rope was in his hands.

He hugged it to his chest and kept his arms bent to absorb the inevitable shock when his full weight settled against his grip. The rope swung wildly beneath the helicopter and he could feel the rough fibers burning against his palms. Instinctively, he tried to lock the rappelling line between his feet to ease some of the strain on his upper body, but his shoes clamped together on empty air. He tried again but the rope simply wasn't there.

As his muscles began to burn from the exertion, he risked a glance down, trying to locate the elusive cord. Then, to his utter dismay, he saw an inch-wide strip of electrical tape around an equally short piece of nylon-sheathed rope, poking from just below his clenched fists.

The curse that escaped his lips was snatched away by the wind as the helicopter pirouetted overhead and began to move off, holding the left wingman position in formation with the others. The milling figures on the observation deck shrank into the distance, as the dark emptiness high above the city engulfed him. On the rope above him, one of the commandos was transferring into the open door of the aircraft, while his counterpart was steadily winching himself higher on the line hanging from the opposite side. The forward motion of the helicopter appeared to be causing the paramilitary operators no real difficulty, but for Kismet, literally at the end of his rope, it was like trying to hang onto the slippery tail of a frightened animal. If he couldn't quickly find a way to relieve some of the strain from his arms....

He didn't even want to think about that eventuality. The ferocious wind tore at his clothes and whipped his necktie against his exposed face. He managed to catch the offending article between his teeth, and from that minor triumph there was a spark of inspiration.

He pressed his mouth to his hands and succeeded in trapping the tie under his thumb. Without releasing his death-grip on the rope, he managed to work a loop of the silk fabric around the line, securing it with a half hitch. Once more using his teeth, he twisted the knot until it was tight on the climbing line. Then, with more haste than caution, he released the hold of his right hand and transferred it to the tie. He half-expected his desperate scheme to fail at that moment; the silk would be too slippery to hold or too fragile to bear his weight and he would find himself in a final, fatal free fall. But lady luck threw him a bone; the knot held.

Before the invention of the mechanical ascender, which was essentially a titanium handle with a small cam to lock into place on a rope and slide in only one direction, mountaineers used a more basic method to hold their place on a line: the prussik. The prescribed technique was to tie a length of cord around the belay line in a girth hitch, which could then be loosened and advanced up the rope, while the free ends of the cord were tied into hand or foot loops. Kismet's field-expedient twist of silk was a far cry from anything taught in climbing school, but it was enough to ease some of the strain on his arms.

The flying formation moved diagonally across midtown toward the East River. Kismet could make out the distinctive slab-like dimensions of the UN building looming just to north, and dead ahead, the twinkling lights of vehicle traffic on the massive span of the Williamsburg Bridge. The pilots had dropped the helicopters a few hundred feet since departing the Empire State Building, but the increasing airspeed suggested that the final destination lay somewhere on the other side of the river. Even with his improvised handhold, he could not hope to hang on to the rope much longer. He had to get inside the helicopter.

He relaxed his hold on the knot and shoved it up the rope until his arm was fully extended. The makeshift prussik made the task easier, but it still took raw muscle strength to make the climb. In a matter of seconds however, he had progressed far enough to wrap the line around one of his legs and lock it in place between his feet, and for the first time in what seemed an eternity of effort, he was able to rest first his right, then his left arm.

The victory was short lived. Thirty feet away, framed in the open door of the helicopter, the commando that had preceded him on the same line was peering down intently. With the wind in his eyes, Kismet couldn't make out any distinctive facial characteristics, but he could see a wicked grin splitting the man's face. With exaggerated slowness, the commando drew an enormous fixed-blade knife from an inverted sheath on his vest and laid the edge against rope.

Kismet lurched into motion, shinnying to the halfway point before the man could complete a single saw stroke, but it wasn't enough. There was no way he was going to reach the helicopter before his foe completed the grim task. On the other rope, the second commando had worked his way to the level of the skids beneath the aircraft and was struggling to pull himself inside.

Kismet released his foothold and arched his back, then kicked at the empty air. His body arced under the tail boom but didn't have enough momentum to reach his objective. He tucked his legs to his chest as the pendulum swung back. Faint tremors rippled through the line as the knife blade split, first the protective sheath, then began parting the braided fibers beneath. Kismet knew he wouldn't get another chance.

As the second arc brought him back under the airframe, he released his grip from the prussik and flailed blindly for the second rope. When the heavy line bounced off his forearm, he curled it to his body and clutched it in his fist. Before he could release the first line however, it went slack then abruptly wrenched him downward; the commando had succeeded in cutting it, and the strands that had moments before been Kismet's only lifeline were now a twenty-pound anchor pulling him toward the murky waters of the East River. He let go without a second thought, and wrapped both his free hand and both legs around the secured rope, but his necktie was still knotted around the untethered line. It yanked hard against his neck, cinching tight both the half hitch around the rope and the four-in-one at his throat.

He struggled with the more immediate threat, the noose around his neck, but could not even insert a finger between the silk swath and his shirt collar. The pressure against his throat was considerable but he could still breathe. Abandoning the idea of freeing himself from the stranglehold, he instead grasped the severed rope and wrapped it loosely around his body.

It was enough for a momentary respite; moments were all he had left.

Without the added security of the prussik, Kismet found himself once more fighting gravity and fatigue. Yet, for all his exhaustion, he was incrementally winning the battle. The underbelly of the helicopter was tangibly close and he could almost touch the landing skids with his fingertips.

A little closer....

A face appeared above him and this time he was near enough to see the beads of perspiration on the man's forehead. The commando's grim smile was not as confident as before, but the determination was still there. So was the knife.

Close enough!

Kismet brought his feet up as high as he dared, clamped them tight on the rope, then thrust his body toward the skid. Although it meant releasing the rope, he stretched out his arms and locked his hands together around the metal frame beneath the helicopter. The commando, busy with trying to cut away the second rope, reacted with a start and fumbled the knife. The glinting steel clattered off the skid mere inches from Kismet's knuckles then vanished into the darkness. An unheard oath crossed the man's lips as he leaned out into the night. Kismet now saw an automatic pistol in his right hand; the barrel was lined up with his head.

"Oh, no you don't!" grated Kismet.

He arched his body again, and like a gymnast on parallel bars, brought his feet up over his head. At the apex of his swing, he brought his legs together, trapping the gun arm between his ankles. He felt a burst of heat through the fabric of his trousers as the weapon discharged and expelled scorching gas against his calf, but that was the limit of injury he sustained from the shot; the bullet whistled away impotently into the night. The gunman didn't get a second chance. With the man's arm still snared, Kismet wrenched himself away and took the commando with him. Realizing too late what his foe was doing, the man flailed desperately at Kismet's leg, but succeeded only in pulling off his left shoe. Then he was gone.

Kismet didn't spare a thought for the falling man; there were still at least two more on the helicopter eager to finish the job their lost comrade had begun, and for his own part, he was still a long way from safety. He wrapped his legs around the skid and repositioned his hands in order to advance toward the door.

The second commando stuck his head and arms through the door, his face a mask of unbridled rage. Despite his fury, which likely stemmed from witnessing the demise of his companion, the man had learned from the mistakes of the other; he lay prone on the deck of the aircraft so that Kismet wouldn't be able to easily knock him from his perch. Cradled in his hands was a compact VZ61 Skorpion machine pistol.

Kismet thrust his head beneath the airframe as 7.65 mm rounds sprayed from the muzzle of the Czech-manufactured weapon. A few of the bullets chattered against landing skids and Kismet could feel vibrations of kinetic energy beneath his fingers. While his current position kept him just barely out of the gunman's line of sight, Kismet had no intention of remaining where he was. The success of his earlier maneuver had bolstered his confidence and the thought of further acrobatics no longer filled him with paralyzing dread. When the gunman fired again, Kismet was nowhere to be seen.

The commando was still peering through the door, searching the night for a glimpse of Kismet's body spiraling down to the a watery fate, when the latter pulled himself through the opposite door and into the relative safety of the helicopter. The pilot caught a glimpse of Kismet and shouted something into the microphone at his lips. The commando, who like the pilot wore a headset, twisted around frantically, but Kismet was faster. He chopped the edge of his hand into the nerve cluster at the base of the gunman's neck then ripped the Skorpion from paralyzed fingers. A second blow, this time with the still smoking barrel of the machine pistol, bludgeoned the man unconscious.

Before the pilot could react, Kismet threaded his way into the cockpit and took the empty seat on the right. He aimed the gun at the pilot and shouted to be heard over the deep thrum of the rotors. "Change of plans!"

The pilot threw him a defiant grin, and then jerked the cyclic control stick to the right. Kismet was just reaching for his tie in order to free himself from the prussik knot, which still bound him to the rope, when the helicopter turned on its side. The Skorpion fell from his grasp as both hands reflexively grabbed for any available handhold, and the discarded weapon smashed into the perspex windscreen, followed an instant later by Kismet himself.

A look of horror contorted the pilot's face as the unmoving form of the second gunman slid through the open hatch and plummeted into the night; his attempt to rattle Kismet had inadvertently sealed the fate of his comrade. Too late, he tried to wrestle the cyclic back in order to level the craft but it refused to budge. It was only then that Kismet realized the object he had grasped, purely as a reflex, was the second control stick, and his weight, now suspended almost vertically from the stick, was holding the helicopter in a fixed bank. The rotor blades narrowly missed the tail boom of the other trailing helicopter in the formation as the out-of-control chopper veered to the south.

Kismet released his hold on the cyclic, and as the pilot righted the aircraft, he dropped easily back into the co-pilot's chair, and in the same motion scooped up the discarded Skorpion and drew a bead on the pilot's forehead. "Let's try that again!"

The man regarded him contemptuously. "If you shoot me, who will fly? You?"

Something about the man's arrogance prompted Kismet to do something admittedly rash. "Why not?"

The pilot's eyes widened in disbelief for an instant as Kismet reached across and clouted him with the barrel of the machine pistol, and then he slumped forward against his harness restraints. Kismet immediately tossed the Skorpion aside and gave his full attention to the redundant control system on his side of the cockpit. Even that brief moment, where the trained pilot's hand had slipped from the cyclic stick, had been enough to permit the helicopter to be knocked off course by the vagaries of wind currents. Kismet steadied the cyclic, while at the same time grasping the collective pitch control stick to his left, and feathered the throttle.

Nick Kismet was not a pilot. While he had flown in helicopters more than a few times and made a point of observing how the crew of those aircraft interacted with their environment, he had only once before, sat in the pilot's seat and that flight, through no fault of his own, had ended very badly. Strangely, he felt no sense of panic, only a grim satisfaction at having wiped the pilot's smile off his face.

"Okay," he muttered. "Time for a refresher course."

He knew the controls: the collective changed the pitch of the rotor blades to adjust lift; the cyclic titled the rotor assembly to bank the aircraft in any direction, or to simply hover; and the foot pedals controlled the rudder. Book knowledge was no substitute for experience, but at least out here in the open air above the river, there was a lot of room for him to get a feel for the unfamiliar systems. At first, his maneuvers were sloppy and erratic, but he quickly learned where only a feather touch was needed and which controls required constant attention.

The other two Jet Rangers had regrouped and were continuing on toward the Brooklyn shore. Kismet hastened to bring his commandeered aircraft back into the formation. Hopefully, the other pilots had no idea that the enemy was in their midst, but Kismet hadn't yet decided how to best exploit that advantage. For now, he just wanted to keep them in sight, especially the one transporting Capri.

The momentary respite from physical activity afforded him a chance to contemplate the events of the evening. While he had no reason to question his original conclusion, namely that his old nemesis Prometheus had emerged from shadows like Leviathan from the sea, there were a few niggling details that he couldn't quite fit into the equation.

He glanced at the unmoving form of the pilot and noted the man's olive complexion and coarse black hair. Every man involved in the operation, at least those he had actually seen, seemed to share a common racial background, but he couldn't put his finger on their shared ethnicity; it had been impossible to discern an accent from the few words he had heard the pilot shout. He stored the information in his memory bank and moved on.

The Skorpion pistols, originally manufactured in the Soviet satellite nation of Czechoslovakia, had been widely distributed among Communist-bloc armies, and subsequent to the fall of the Iron Curtain, had become very popular on the black market. The gun's compact design made it a favorite with urban terrorist cells. He thought back to his singular encounter with Prometheus assassins. Those men had also been well-trained commandos, but had gone to great lengths to conceal their features. Only their leader had revealed his face—a man with fair hair and skin, and a German name. The weapons they had employed had been top of the line, not old Soviet surplus. The discrepancies weren't overwhelming to be sure, but there was a more troubling question that lent significance to those disparate scraps of information. What did they want with Capri Martelli?

The formation had been steadily descending as it moved across the river, so that now the helicopters were only about two hundred feet above the water. On the Brooklyn shore, Kismet could make out the industrial environs of the old naval yard; a maze of warehouses and cranes that had once been the foremost construction facility for American warships but was now a private concern. As the approach continued, he saw a cluster of black vans ringing an open space on a large wooden pier, an area just large enough for three helicopters to land.

He stared intently at the tableau, searching for some way to take control of the situation. He did not doubt that Capri's abductors would have reinforcements waiting in those vans, further stacking the odds against him. If he was going to have a chance at rescuing her, he would have to force that helicopter to land somewhere else.

But how do you force a helicopter down? He saw the answer almost as soon as the thought formed, and groaned. But he had already used up more lives than a cat since meeting Capri; what was one more?

He pushed the cyclic forward, accelerating the helicopter until he was practically kissing the tail rotor of the lead aircraft, the one with Capri. It was impossible to see the blades as they knifed through the air, providing lateral stability to counteract the torque generated by the main rotor, but they were there nonetheless. He held that distance for a moment, steeling himself against what he was about to do. If the pilot at the head of the formation knew that Kismet was in control of the helicopter that was sidling closer, he gave no indication; the Jet Ranger stayed on course, descending and decelerating steadily. Kismet matched his movements, and then abruptly moved even closer, leading the target.

When the time came, he did not hesitate. He stomped one of the rudder pedals, and the helicopter pirouetted on its axis. The tail boom whipped around violently and the steering rotor of Kismet's helicopter met the tail assembly of the lead chopper in a collision of metal. An awful shudder and a noise like a train wreck, rippled through both aircraft as the tail rotors annihilated each other in an explosion of shrapnel. The helicopter lurched, as if abruptly coming to a halt, then began to spin violently as torque from the main rotor whipped the fuselage in the opposite direction. For just an instant, Kismet saw the shattered remains of the lead helicopter's tail boom began to whip sideways, then everything became a blur of motion.

He was ready for the loss of control and

immediately increased both pitch and throttle, and then pushed forward on the cyclic. At first, his wounded aircraft corkscrewed through the air, dropping lower with each circuit. Then, as his airspeed grudgingly increased, the helicopter began to stabilize. At sixty knots, the wind of his passage through the air was enough to hold the airframe steady beneath the rotor, like a weather vane in a stiff breeze. It took a moment longer for Kismet, still reeling from the dizzying spirals, to ascertain that the pilot of the other helicopter had emulated his movements and was currently charting almost the same course away from the naval yard, a northeast vector that had already passed the Williamsburg Bridge and would shortly take them into the borough of Queens.

He eased off the cyclic just enough to let the other helicopter pull ahead. Although he had prevented the kidnappers from making their rendezvous, they were still calling the shots. Kismet would have to wait and see where the pilot decided to put down; only then would he have a chance at liberating Capri. Admittedly, not a great chance, but maybe the only one she would get.

The pilot of the lead chopper wasted no time finding an open area to set down. Kismet saw, to his chagrin, that the new course was heading toward a rail bed where several lines from the Long Island Railroad formed a junction. It was one of the few areas in the massive New York transit network where the tracks did not run either on elevated platforms or through subterranean tunnels. While the area was clear of buildings, it was cris-crossed with a web of virtually invisible overhead power lines. While an expert pilot might be able to guide a disabled helicopter through the net, Kismet would be hard pressed to make any sort of landing. He racked his brain to remember the steps for a controlled "hard landing"--pilot-speak for a crash.

The first Jet Ranger lined up on the rails as it descended, and when its landing assembly was almost kissing the tracks, the pilot pulled back on the cyclic. The fuselage immediately began to slough sideways, but an instant later the skids touched down. The helicopter started to whip around in a shower of sparks, but the friction of contact rapidly cancelled out the torque forces. After spinning three tight circles, the fuselage ground to a halt, while the main rotor began winding down.

Kismet knew he didn't have a prayer of imitating the other pilot's landing; he simply wasn't familiar enough with the aircraft to achieve the sort of instantaneous response to the vagaries of an emergency descent. But like it or not, he had to put the stricken helicopter on the ground. He swooped down toward the rails, threading between the power lines, and when he thought he was low enough, straightened the stick and throttled off.

The helicopter instantly began to auto-rotate; the fuselage spun in the opposite direction of the rotor blades, reducing its lift to almost nothing. The airframe slammed into the tracks with a force that shook Kismet's hands from the controls. The Jet Ranger's forward momentum sent it like a runaway train toward the first aircraft, and there was nothing he could do to stop it. Then one of the rotor blades clipped the ground and all hell broke loose.

The Jet Ranger came apart, flinging parts in every direction, as it began rolling end over end down the tracks. Shattered fragments of the rotors slammed into the parked helicopter like guided missiles and knocked it on its side, triggering a similar catastrophe as that aircraft's main rotor slammed into the ground, one vane at a time. An instant later, the two demolished aircraft embraced in a spectacular collision, throwing fragments of metal and plastic confetti in a lethal shower. A fifty-yard section of the rail line was plowed up, strewn with wreckage before the twisted ruin finally came to rest.

At the heart of the storm, Kismet had escaped injury from flying shrapnel, but was nevertheless disoriented from the centrifugal and kinetic forces generated by the crash landing. Even after physical motion had ceased, everything in his world continued spinning for several seconds. When he was certain that he had suffered no mortal injury, he gingerly extricated himself from the wreckage. As soon as his legs were free of the crumpled cockpit panels, he dropped from his seat and spilled out onto the debris-strewn ground. Until his fall, he had not even realized that the wreck had left him hanging upside down.

After finally wrestling free of his necktie and the rope to which it was anchored, he cautiously approached the ruins of the second helicopter. An oily smell pervaded the air and a plume of smoke was rising from the engine cowling. It had not been his intention to demolish the aircraft and as the scope of the devastation hit him, he felt a pang of guilt; in attempting to save Capri, he might very well have killed her. A stream of blood trickled from beneath the twisted sculpture of destruction; a long shard of metal, probably one of the rotor blades from Kismet's chopper, had spitted the fuselage. With growing dread, he began tearing at the panels and like a grim surgeon, exposed the gory mess within.

Despite the carnage, he experienced a moment of

relief. The barely recognizable form impaled on the rotor vane wore high-top basketball shoes, not stiletto heels. The next human form he encountered, though bruised and unmoving, was still alive but it wasn't Capri; he kept digging. Deep within the shattered airframe, his hands closed on a piece of aluminum tubing, and when he pulled it free, he saw her.

Capri was still unconscious and still secured within the Stokes litter. Although her expensive suit was stained with blood and grease, she appeared to be uninjured; her impromptu cage had afforded her an additional level of protection during the crash, and the sedative in her bloodstream had relaxed her muscles, further sparing her from injury. Kismet loosened the straps and pulled her away from the smoldering wreck. Once in the clear, he slipped an arm under her knees and lifted her off the ground. She wasn't heavy--with a fashion model's physique, she probably weighed a hundred pounds soaking wet--but Kismet's muscles were exhausted beyond fatigue. His legs felt like lead, and although he was trying to run from the scene of the dual aircraft collision, he appeared to merely stagger.

Sirens were audible in the distance, but the familiar thump of rotor blades gradually drowned out the shrill noise of approaching emergency vehicles. The third helicopter was on its way and Kismet knew his enemies would arrive before the police. He had to get Capri away from the train line, away from anywhere her kidnappers might think to look. Every step was an ordeal.

Suddenly there was a figure standing directly in his path. Kismet fell to his knees and croaked: "Help me!" But even as the words escaped his lips, he knew that this shadowy presence was not there to offer aid.

He wore the cassock of a monk, with a cowl that completely hid his face. In different circumstances, Kismet would have thought the costume ostentatious, even laughable, but there was something strangely authentic--and deeply malefic--about the vestments. As the figure began to approach, Kismet noticed a length of black rope tied around his waist like a sash, and depending from one of the ends was a crucifix of carved wood, but for some reason, the short end of the vertical post was pointing toward the ground; the cross was inverted.

Kismet's blood ran cold. He tried to get up, to lift Capri and resume their flight to freedom, but she had grown impossibly heavy. The dark monk glided closer, as if his unseen feet were floating above the ground. Kismet laid his charge aside as gently as possible, and then struggled to his feet.

He's just a man; just an ordinary flesh and blood human, who happens to believe that he's got help from below. Well, I know better.

He struck a fighter's stance and waited for the malevolent figure to get within range. Although the man was almost in reach, his face remained a blank shadow beneath his hood, the same lightless hue as the cord around his waist. Kismet took a swing.

A robed arm shot out to block the punch, and as the gnarled fingers brushed his hand aside, Kismet felt something like an electrical shock course through his entire body. When he raised his head a moment later, he found that he had been knocked backward a dozen steps. In the periphery of his vision, he saw a pair of figures--two of the men that had first kidnapped Capri--approaching her motionless form, but then his attention was consumed by the baleful entity steadily advancing toward him. Before he could rise or retreat, his foe was upon him.

Frail ancient fingers, impossibly strong, closed around his throat and began to squeeze. Kismet fought the killing grip and directed impotent blows against the monk's head and body, all to no avail. He caught a glimpse of Capri, dragged by her captors back to the surviving helicopter, but then his world was consumed by darkness... except for a single piercing beam of light, shining like the sun, and drawing him closer.

Then the dark monk was gone.

Nick Kismet lay spread-eagled across the parallel tracks of the Long Island Railroad, illuminated by the headlights of an onrushing train.

3

They smoke cigars in heaven?

It was an odd thought, since Kismet didn't particularly believe in the afterlife. Nevertheless, the air was heavy with the sweet but acrid scent of burning tobacco. He started to open his eyes, but then a railroad spike of pain shot through his skull and he retreated into unconsciousness again.

"Cuban?" he muttered abruptly. He had no idea how much time had passed, but this time he wisely kept his eyes shut. It didn't help much.

A dry chuckle rattled inside his head. "Why, Lieutenant Kismet, that would be illegal."

Despite the incessant hammers ringing against the anvil of his skull, Kismet opened his eyes to investigate. He was in a small, relatively dark place, sprawled out on a couch upholstered in soft leather; it was, he realized, the interior of a limousine. Three men were sitting on a matching divan directly across from where he lay, surrounded by a halo of smoke, which issued from the phallic cigar jutting from the mouth of the man in the center. Of the trio, he was the most distinguished; his suit was a dark three-piece Saville Row, and a diamond studded Rolex encircled his wrist, but even if his adornments were discounted, the man still looked impressive, with chiseled features and a magnificent mane of silver hair. "Well, I guess you aren't God," Kismet said, at length. "He would know that I resigned my commission years ago. Which means I'm still alive, right?"

The man with the cigar laughed again then spoke in a deep basso profundo. "My apologies, Mr. Kismet. I wish I could say that my information about you was just outdated, but the truth is that I was hoping to appeal to your sense of *esprit de corp.*"

Something about the man was familiar, but Kismet's mental energies were taxed to their limits just to stay conscious. He couldn't help but notice the underlying accent, and the faint trace of a New Jersey accent , which was all the more incongruous when spoken in a voice so low as to be almost a growl. "I don't follow you."

"I was a soldier, too. A different war, but I fought for my country all the same."

Kismet was beginning to feel like Alice, waking up in someone else's dream. He forced himself to sit up. "What country was that?"

The man ignored his question, but seemed impressed at his resilience. "We thought you were dead--"

"So did I."

"—but Sally just managed to pull you off the tracks before that train sliced you up for fish bait."

It was the first thing he'd heard that made any kind of sense. "Tell Sally I said thanks."

"You're welcome," grunted the man on the right, an imposing figure cut from the same cloth as the two men that had been shadowing Capri on the observation deck.

Comprehension washed over Kismet like the waves of a rising tide. "Okay, that was almost an introduction. What should I call you? Godfather?"

The two men on his flank bristled warily, but their leader raised a hand. "That's not necessary. I am Giovanni Turino; most of my friends just call me Joe."

"Yeah? Well, I'm not real keen on getting into your social network Giovanni." If Turino was rankled by his answer he gave no indication, but Sal and the other bodyguard seemed to turn purple in the low light. He ignored their ire and continued. "And while I appreciate you guys pulling my bacon out of the fire back there, something tells me your appearance on the scene wasn't a coincidence."

"You're very astute, Mr. Kismet. Capri is my granddaughter."

"Ah, well that almost explains everything." He already suspected as much, based on the girl's earlier reference. No doubt the mob boss had the resources to check up on all of his granddaughter's social engagements. But as soon as he allowed that thought to sink in, a new can of worms was opened. He thought about the dark monk with the Satanic cross: *Was that real? And what does any of this have to do with Prometheus?* "So is this some kind of turf war?"

A corner of Turino's mouth twitched, but rather than answer, he turned to Sal. "Get our guest something to drink. Something for the pain, eh?"

Sal twisted in his seat and opened the cabinet doors to reveal a well-stocked bar. "What's your pleasure?"

Kismet almost demurred then reconsidered when he spied a sixteen-year-old single malt. Eager to show his independence, he took hold of the bottle and decanted a double portion for himself. There was a bucket of ice in the bar, but he took it neat and drained the glass in a long gulp.

Sal passed his employer a tumbler with equal parts of the amber liquor and water. Turino took a sip and smiled approvingly. "A good choice, but if you're going to swill it down like that, you might want to stick with vodka. Less chance of a hangover."

Kismet spent a moment enjoying the warm glow that spread from his chest to his extremities, before replying. "Thanks for the tip. Now, unless you're going to tell me what's going on, I'd appreciate if you could just drop me…" He glanced out the window, but saw nothing familiar in the endless urban landscape. "Just let me out at the next light."

Turino regarded him through eyes that had narrowed into defensive slits. "You asked if this was a turf war; that's exactly what it is, Mr. Kismet. And they've dragged my granddaughter into it."

"You have my sympathy but, forgive me for saying this, I thought that sort of stuff went with the territory."

"I don't expect you to approve of, or even understand, my life," Turino rumbled. "But Capri is an innocent."

"Let me guess. She thinks you're a successful…what, plumber? Building contractor? And you no doubt play the part of doting grandfather."

"Capri has no illusions about me, Mr. Kismet. But she has earned the right to judge; her parents…my beloved daughter, God rest her soul, and her husband were killed when she was just a girl. She wanted nothing to do with the family business, and I made sure she didn't have to."

Kismet poured himself another scotch whisky. Despite his ambivalent facade, he was curious about Capri's background, and eager for clues that might expose the identity of the men that had kidnapped her. "You got her a cushy job writing for that rag, the *Clarion*?"

"She got the job on her own merits. In fact, she is a much better journalist than they deserve. I'm afraid the editors at the Times were as quick to judge as you are."

"Okay, so she's innocent. I did everything I could to save her--"

"For which I am grateful." The capo leaned forward. "You may not like what I am, but be sure of this: my gratitude means something."

Kismet nodded. "Fine, but why am I still here?"

Turino started to answer, then sat back and took a long pull on the cigar. He closed his eyes as he exhaled. "He almost killed you, didn't he."

"What?"

"Negron, the dark priest. He was there, right?"

"There wasn't exactly a formal introduction." Kismet winced at the memory and his hands unconsciously went to his throat. "Negron, huh? He seemed a little theatrical for an up and coming mob boss."

"He's much more than that. Negron is no ordinary priest."

"I kind of picked up on that. Let me guess: he worships the Devil?"

The bodyguards shifted nervously and Sal crossed himself. Turino squinted again. "Are you familiar with the Vatican archives?"

"I understand they have an unparalleled collection of erotica," Kismet said with a straight face.

Turino barked a short, humorless laugh. "For centuries, the Vatican has hoarded the world's largest collection of art, historical documents, religious artifacts and so on. For the most part, the catalog has remained a closely guarded secret, even to those within the Church. But back in the late 1800's the Pope decided to open the archive to examination by scholars and members of the clergy. One of those scholars was a Benedictine monk visiting from Bogotá who was researching the Holy Relics of the Crucifixion. His name was Brother Emilio Negron."

Kismet bit back a skeptical reply. He remained

curious as to the connection the Mafia Don would make between the Vatican archives and the kidnapping of his granddaughter, but more than that, the mention of the capital city of the Republic of Colombia had struck a chord; the kidnappers uniform racial characteristics could be indicative of a common Latin American background. Turino seemed to be waiting for a response, so Kismet nodded. "Go on."

"You are familiar with the relics of Christ? You deal with that sort of thing, right?"

"Splinters from the True Cross; the nails that pierced Jesus' hands and feet; burial shrouds." He shook his head. "Among other things, my office deals with historic art treasures from ancient civilizations. Religious artifacts typically have a dubious pedigree, and if you'll pardon my candor, they're a dime a dozen."

There was a noncommittal grunt. "Brother Emilio found several of the items you've mentioned. But there was something else buried deep within the repository; something that was never meant to be revealed. Negron called it 'the Judas Rope.'"

"According to the Bible, Judas Iscariot committed suicide after betraying Jesus. The Gospel of Matthew says he hanged himself." Kismet flashed back to the dark cord that had been tied like a sash around the monk's cassock. "Somebody kept the rope?"

"There is no official record to support that; only Negron's supposition."

Kismet folded his arms. "On the other hand, the book of Acts records that Judas jumped off a cliff and splattered himself all over the rocks. No rope. It's one of many contradictions in scripture."

"I'm not here to debate apologetics," snapped Turino. It was the first time he had shown the slightest bit of irritation. "Whether or not you believe in these relics, or even in the teachings of the Church, this man Negron does believe."

Kismet was unbowed. "Fine. He was a true believer. Now tell me how he ends up working for the guy downstairs."

"Judas was seduced by avarice, one of the seven deadly sins. He was stealing from the poor box, and when he decided to betray the Christ, it was for money. But after the crucifixion, he felt remorse. He was so distraught he decided to take his own life. He tried to hang himself, but the rope broke and his body fell onto the rocks." Turino took a deep breath. "Now, that is what the apologists say. Negron came to a different conclusion.

"When Judas betrayed the Christ with a kiss, he was damned, beyond hope of forgiveness. Even so, when he realized what he had done, he wanted to take it back. He threw the blood money into the temple, but it wasn't enough. So he took a rope, tied it to a tree and tried to kill himself, as if his suicide—a mortal sin by itself—might balance scales and erase his eternal damnation. But the Devil knows when you try to renege on your deal. The rope broke and Judas died an accidental death. He was denied absolution from his crime and his black soul stained the rope noose around his neck. Brother Emilio believed that rope had become an unholy relic, wholly evil. Anyone touching it would be seduced into the service of Satan. No one is sure why, but after he figured all this out, Negron took the rope and vanished. He was subsequently excommunicated and sentenced to death in absentia by the Inquisition."

"And he's still alive over a century later?"

"I guess Lucifer actually kept his end of the

bargain. As long as the servant remains faithful to his master, he is blessed with unending life."

"Longevity doesn't seem to agree with Brother Emilio." Kismet stroked his chin thoughtfully. "Did you know that the Church invented Satanism? No one was worshiping the Devil until the Holy Inquisition decided it needed a pretext for persecuting its political enemies. The Black Mass, the rites and symbols, backwards Latin...all trumped up by so-called witnesses in order to condemn people who didn't conform to the narrow interpretation of the faith or bow to the absolute power of the Church. If Negron believed that rope made people want to worship the devil, then it was his own belief that made it happen."

Turino gazed at him, his face unreadable.

"Let's say I accept everything you've said," continued Kismet. "How does this involve you? And Capri?"

"Greed, Mr. Kismet. The sin of Judas. It is what drives Negron, even today." Turino stubbed out his cigar. "For over a hundred years, Negron has roamed the world looking for acolytes to join him on the dark path. In the last few years, he has returned to the nation of his birth, and embraced a new generation of followers."

"The drug cartels."

Turino nodded. "One by one, he has corrupted the cartel drug lords to the path of evil."

"Not exactly a long trip," observed Kismet.

"It is one thing to compel a man to break the laws of nations. But to make them forsake God? That is not so easily done."

"So how did he do it?"

"With the rope. He doesn't threaten them directly. Such a forced conversion would have no value.

Instead, he threatens to kill their loved ones with the Judas Rope. If someone dies with the rope around their neck, they are eternally damned. The cartel barons were given a choice: swear allegiance to Negron, or their loved ones will burn forever. If they ever break their oath, the curse is binding. Once he ruled the cartels, Negron had an army at his disposal, and like any victorious king, set his sights on a bigger prize: the American syndicates."

Kismet found this even less credible than the notion of a devil-worshiping immortal priest. "So criminals and murderers are worried about their eternal souls?"

"We care about our families, Mr. Kismet." Turino's voice had become as taut as a garrote. "I won't waste my breath trying to explain our code to you, our sense of honor, but ours is a tradition that goes back hundreds of years. The Colombians may be animals, savage and vicious, but they still protect the ones they love. And we share something else: faith.

"You call us criminals, murderers...you have no idea. We have always walked a fine line between belief and damnation. Threaten my eternal soul..." He made a dismissive gesture. "But that doesn't mean I don't believe. Now, you make that threat against my beloved granddaughter and you'll get my attention. Give me the choice between my own soul and hers, that's easy."

Kismet kept his expression hard. "Do you believe Negron has this power?"

"It doesn't matter what I believe. He has her, and if I don't do what he says, he'll kill her."

Then the last piece of the puzzle clicked into place. "You want me to rescue her."

A guilty look softened the Mafioso's countenance. "Negron is holding Capri at a house in Montauk. If

I'm not standing in front of him by midnight, to swear on the Judas Rope to serve him and his master, he'll kill her. That's three hours from now, Mr. Kismet. My men told me what happened at the Empire State Building. And I saw you fight Negron with my own eyes. If anyone can help her, it's you."

Kismet looked away, gazing through the tinted windows at the streetlights and storefronts as they passed by. He realized with a start that the chauffeur had navigated through city streets to the Brooklyn Heights neighborhood where Kismet lived. The Don was giving him a choice. He turned his gaze back to Turino. "I'll need to get a few things first."

Kismet did not linger to watch the limousine continue down the wooded drive; his attention was already fixed on the task at hand, namely navigating through the dark pine forest at a brisk walk. After a few minutes, his eyes adjusted to the near total absence of light and he was able to increase his pace to a jog. At first, the muscle aches from injuries incurred earlier in the night were almost debilitating, but as he moved, exercising the stiffness from his limbs, the pain became more tolerable; the Motrin tablets he had downed probably helped too.

During the two-hour ride across Long Island, he had struggled to devise a strategy for rescuing Capri. Fortunately, the property currently being used by Negron and his minions was listed with a real estate broker, and floor plans and a full map of the estate were available on a realtor's market listing service. It was a marginal piece of intelligence but Kismet knew he was going to need every advantage to survive the night.

The forty room mansion was situated above the

Atlantic Ocean and separated from the main road by several hundred acres of woodland, through which ran an elaborate maze of horse trails. There were several satellite buildings, including a stable, an enormous garage with a coach house, and a full-fledged guesthouse, but Kismet felt certain Capri would be kept in the main residence, probably in one of the bedrooms that overlooked the surf. He had outlined his plan to Turino during the ride, and the capo had given a guarded blessing.

"I won't be able to help you. I'm going to have to go in there like he's beaten me, 'cause if you fail, I'll have no choice but to do what he wants." Turino had grabbed his forearm meaningfully. "Don't fail. Once you're clear, call my cell phone; it's set to vibrate, so no one will hear. When you give the signal, I'll pull out. If necessary, I'll come out shooting. And there'll be two cars of my guys waiting just outside the gate. They have phones programmed for the same number, so they'll move as soon as you make the call."

Now, as he reached the edge of the woods, Kismet could see Turinos's car as it rolled to a halt in front of the marble stairs leading up into the main house. Several men wearing casual clothes and openly displaying assault weapons surrounded the vehicle. Turino was ushered up the steps, while his bodyguards remained where they were. Kismet frowned, but this development was not entirely unexpected.

He skirted along the edge of the woods toward the east end of the house. His quick surveillance led him to believe that Negron's men were not vigorously patrolling the grounds; they probably didn't have the manpower, and confident in their leader's omnipotence, must have reckoned themselves secure enough with guards at the main gate and the front door. If he was wrong, and Negron's men had state of the art video monitors and motion sensors, then he would find out very soon. He eased from the woods and moved smoothly across the open expanse between the forest and the house. Once safely behind the screen of topiary that ringed the perimeter, he hastened to the rear of the house, perched high above the roaring ocean. There was not a soul to be seen.

"So far, so good."

The mansion had been designed to resemble a medieval castle, but the stonework on its mock battlements had sacrificed security for aesthetic appeal. The craggy surface presented no obstacle to Kismet as he climbed up to the level of the second floor balcony. Several sets of French doors opened onto the long terrace, but without exception, the glass panes were dark; no lights were visible in the bank of apartments where he expected to find Capri held hostage. After a quick reconnaissance, he returned to the first door and examined the lock. There was no keyhole to operate the mechanism and the bolt was hidden behind a thin strip of wood.

Frowning, Kismet reached into the black nylon waist pack--one of the items he had secured from his residence before making the long drive to Montauk, along with a change of clothes--and produced his *kukri*. The large chopping knife, which could almost be described as a short sword, was the signature weapon of the Gurkhas, a British infantry regiment originally drawn from a fierce Nepalese warrior tribe of the same name. The knife was a memento of war, given to him by one of the men that had fought at his side on the night of his initial encounter with the assassins of Prometheus, but was no less practical for all its sentimental value. The boomerang shaped blade, nearly fifteen inches in length, could be used like an axe, a shovel, or in this case, a pry bar. He slid the point of the knife under the fascia strip and twisted. The wood splintered to reveal the thick lock bolt underneath. The kukri made quick work of the bolt as well, and a few moments later, the door swung silently open.

He exchanged the knife for his Glock 17 automatic pistol, then moved inside. The room beyond was empty. A thin stripe of light peeked from beneath the interior door, and Kismet dropped to a prone position in order to peek through the tiny crack. There was no movement in the corridor beyond, nor any sound of voices, but his field of view was limited to the opposite side of the hallway. After taking a deep breath, he gently turned the door handle and eased the solid wood door open a few millimeters. The hallway, like the room, was as empty as a tomb.

The complete absence of any activity gave him pause; perhaps he had erred in assuming that Capri would be held in one of the apartments. If she wasn't there, then his plan to rescue her without raising an alarm was out the window. He crept down the corridor and crouched at the end of an ornate balustrade, which partitioned the landing above a sweeping staircase down to the main level. Voices were wafting up from below and he strained to comprehend what was being said.

Turino's baritone thundered above the others. His stentorian volume was intentional; it was his way of keeping Kismet abreast of developments. The mafia leader was presently stalling by making outrageous demands of his Colombian hosts. The thin voices of the men giving answers suggested that the dark monk was not present; there was still a chance to pull this off.

"I'm through with your games," Turino roared. "If my granddaughter isn't standing in front of me in two minutes, I'm walking out of here."

Kismet's frown deepened. He could just make out two of the Colombian's conversing in Spanish. "*Bring the girl out to the top of the stairs.*"

Kismet scrambled back from the banister. So Capri was upstairs. But now he had about ninety seconds in which to find her and escape, at which point the alarm would be sounded. He swore under his breath and glanced at the uniform doors that lined the hallway. Reasoning that her kidnappers were too lazy to drag her unconscious form any farther than they had to, he crept to the door closest to the landing. There was a deadbolt lock on the door, but when he tried the lever the latch yielded and he hastened into the darkened room. In the instant before he closed the door, ambient light from without illuminated a motionless form, bound and gagged, resting against a wall. He had found her, but how long before the Colombians found him? He needed a diversion, something--anything--to distract the man presently ascending the steps.

Then it hit him. He dug out the cell phone, and without a second thought, punched the send button.

In the instant in which Turino abruptly announced that he was done waiting and turned toward the door, two Lincoln Continentals filled with heavily armed men, each fiercely loyal to the Family, burst through the wrought iron main gate in a shower of sparks and an explosion of gunfire. Although the Colombians in the gatehouse were armed with semi-automatic assault rifles and machine pistols, the Mafiosi had the element of surprise on their side. The gate guards went down under a hail of .38 and .44 caliber rounds without getting off a shot or making any kind of call for help.

Nevertheless, the thunder of gunfire echoed across the estate, raising the alarm as effectively as a klaxon. Negron's men, wherever they were on the property, came instantly alert and brought their weapons to the ready, looking for someone to kill. On the steps inside the house, the man coming up to retrieve Capri paused and looked back to his immediate superior for further guidance. In those few indecisive seconds, Turino reached the front door, where he drew a snub-nosed .38 revolver from an ankle holster and broke into a run. The Colombians managed to throw off their confused hesitancy and rushed to stop him, but the moment they crossed the threshold, Turino's limousine skidded to a halt in front of the steps, and the mobster's confederates emerged with weapons cocked and locked. The war had begun.

Kismet sliced Capri's bonds and removed the gag before trying to rouse her. He had no way of knowing if his premature signal to Turino had accomplished the sole purpose of distracting the man coming up the stairs, but there was no mistaking the sound of gunshots, both in the distance and nearby. As he shook the unconscious girl's shoulder with his left hand, the Glock was fixed in his right.

She came awake in a narcotic stupor, alternately drowsy, shivering and nauseous. Her lethargy left Kismet feeling frustrated and helpless. "Capri, honey, wake up. We're in trouble here."

"Who...?"

"It's Nick. You've got to pull it together, Capri. I need you back on your feet."

Her reply was still groggy. "Nick... Kismet? I

was... what happened?"

"Long story. The short version is that you were kidnapped and I'm here to rescue you." He clenched his teeth to dam his rising ire. "Can you stand?"

He could feel her shaking in his grasp, but she answered in the affirmative. He guided her to the balcony doors and pushed through out into the night. The noise of gunfire was muted on the oceanward side of the house. Kismet approached the parapet cautiously, but there was no activity below. "I'm going to lower you down, okay?"

She nodded dumbly. Evidently the soporific in her bloodstream had left her numb to fear and anxiety. He lifted her onto the banister rail then grasped her forearms. At the last instant, she jerked like a live wire in his hands and slipped free, but Kismet has already lowered her to where she was only a couple feet above the manicured lawn and the springy grass gently received her without so much as a stumble. Kismet landed beside her then immediately caught her hand and steered her toward the woods. They had almost reached the dense forest when a new noise cut through the night: dogs.

Kismet snapped a quick glance over his shoulder. Four sinewy shapes bolted from the front of the house, emitting sharp barks and low growls as they ran. Their lean silhouettes and dark coats marked them as Dobermans, a fierce but loyal German breed and cousin to the beefier, but similarly colored Rottweiler. Dobermans were often used by police and security forces as patrol dogs, and as such were trained to attack. Yet it was not the dogs Kismet was most worried about, but rather their human handlers, who were no doubt closely observing where the canines were going. He debated making a stand, shooting the dogs as they charged, but thought better of it; he'd probably miss, and the shots would just draw more attention to their presence. But one thing was certain: if they went into the forest, the dogs would run them down.

"Change of plans!" He turned so abruptly that Capri, still clinging to his left hand, was whipped violently onto the new course. They now moved parallel to the wooded area, toward a cluster of small structures. Kismet racked his brain to remember which was the one he wanted. Meanwhile, the dog pack was closing. He decided the closest one was good enough.

As with the main residence, faux medieval was the dominant theme for the satellite buildings. A heavy door of vertical planks, studded with wrought iron strap hinges, secured the structure to which they now hastened. Kismet counted down his steps and when he reached zero, launched himself feet first at the door. The solid oak bounced him back without yielding a millimeter. He rebounded, landing on his feet, and whirled, with the Glock in one hand and his kukri in the other, to face the inevitable onslaught.

"Nick!" Capri screamed.

He ignored her. With four ferocious slavering beasts about to rip into them, the last thing he needed was to have to keep the nearly catatonic journalist apprised of every little development.

"Nick, it's open!"

The words sank in with agonizing slowness, and his mute disbelief would have proved fatal if Capri had not grasped his elbow and yanked him through the open portal. He recovered his senses enough to slam the door shut and throw the heavy slide bolt. He could hear the Dobermans scratching at the planks.

"It wasn't locked," she explained in a more subdued voice.

He shook his head in amazement. "Looks like I owe you one."

She offered a wry smile. Her eyes were still slightly glazed, but she seemed otherwise lucid. "I think it's more like this evens the score, but if you want, you can buy me a drink later and explain just what the hell is going on. Just tell me one thing: is it Prometheus?"

"Nothing so mundane. This one is the devil you know." As he led her away from the door, he quickly related everything he had learned from Turino. The first time he mentioned her grandfather, he sensed embarrassment but he did not give her an opportunity to posture herself as an unwilling member of the crime family, and when the tale turned to satanic monks and unholy relics, her discomfort was forgotten.

"Do you believe any of this?"

"I believe there are some pretty ruthless bad guys who don't want to let us leave. And the guy leading them is..." He trailed off as they pushed through an interior door to reveal a vast garage, housing several recreational vehicles. In between a twenty-foot ski boat and a brace of Bombardier four wheeled all-terrain vehicles, was a Honda XR650R Enduro motorcycle. The Enduro was a street legal bike designed for off road use, which in simple terms meant that in addition to its heavy-duty suspension and knobby tires, it was equipped with head and tail lights. "I think we just got lucky."

He had no sooner uttered the words than the harsh crack of gunfire broke the relative stillness inside the garage. Someone was shooting through the door. Capri grimaced at the sound. "You were saying?"

4

The door exploded open and instantly, in a flurry of snapping jaws, the dog pack rushed into the outer hallway. The gunman who had shot the lock open lingered cautiously out of view, but when the expected retort of gunfire did not occur, he edged beneath the lintel.

Kismet hit a switch and bathed the hallway in the glare of the Enduro's headlight. He and Capri had rolled the motorcycle into the hallway and hid behind the open door long enough to misdirect the Dobermans. Now, with Capri's arms around his waist and the Colombian transfixed in the blinding beam of light, Kismet stomped on the kick-starter.

The engine sputtered weakly but did not engage.

No problem. Sometimes it takes a few tries to catch. He pushed the starter again… and again.

The gunman, still shading his eyes with one hand, raised the gun and fired blind. The concussion of the discharge thundered in the narrow confines of the hallway. Kismet reflexively ducked and in the same motion, flicked the lights off. After the harsh illumination, the darkness engulfing the small enclosure was all the more profound, punctuated only by the muzzle flash of the Colombian's machine pistol. Kismet felt something slap his left arm, followed by a blossom of pain. He tried not to think about it.

Suddenly, the engine caught and the roar of the motorcycle drowned out the sound of gunfire. Kismet squeezed the front brake and let the rear tire spin until the smell of burnt rubber overpowered the stench of cordite. "Hang on!"

He let go of the brake and the Enduro shot

forward. There was a sickening crunch as the bike struck something, then rolled up and over whatever it was. Kismet didn't need the light to know what he had hit, but once they were out in the open air, he switched it on anyway.

Sporadic gunfire was still echoing over the treetops, but the ferocity of the initial attack had faltered. The paved drive beckoned enticingly, a two-mile ribbon of smooth road that could deliver them to safety in a matter of minutes, but Kismet instead steered back toward the tree line. The driveway was well lit and would almost certainly be a focus for the Colombian gunmen as they mounted their counterattack. Navigating the horse trails through the forest might take a good while longer, but hopefully it would spare them a trip through the gauntlet.

A path, lined with wood chips, marked the way from the stables to an open field where a steeplechase course had been laid out, and continued around the perimeter to woods beyond. The exercise area was less well kept than the grounds around the house; evidently the current tenants' hobbies did not extend to equestrian activities. Kismet opened up the throttle to make the crossing as quickly as possible; he knew he would have to proceed more slowly in the woods.

He winced when Capri gripped his biceps, and only then did he realize that she had been shouting something. "What?"

"You're hurt!" Her small voice was barely audible over the roar of the engine.

"It's just a scratch! What's wrong?"

"They're coming!"

He risked a quick glance over his shoulder and saw two separate sets of bobbing headlights in the vicinity of the garage they had just exited--the quad ATVs.

Less distinct were four smaller shapes, moving alongside the vehicles. Kismet bit off a curse as he swung his attention forward and geared down to enter the forest.

The trail started off straight and broad and dived quickly into the heart of the woods, but after a quarter of a mile, the path began to shrink and the canopy of branches drooped down like threatening tentacles. After the first turn, they could no longer discern the glare of lights from the pursuing quads. That was the good news. The bad news was that the trail was deeply rutted, which not only forced him to further reduce his speed, but also revealed that the trail had been used extensively by off-road vehicles. The Colombians had been entertaining themselves during their stay by exploring the horse trails with the ATVs, so there was a good chance that the men chasing them knew these trails well.

Before long, they began to descend along a trail that cut across a hillside which formed one wall of a deep ravine. It was a single track, barely wide enough to accommodate the motorcycle, and Kismet was hopeful that the ATV riders wouldn't be able to follow. At the bottom of the slope, he glanced back to see if their pursuers were still on the hunt, but saw nothing. Somehow, the lack of activity was more troubling than if the Colombians had come charging down the hill. In the absence of any other option, he gunned the bike up the opposite side of the gully.

They were waiting for him at the top.

The Colombians had killed their lights and set an ambush. Their intimate familiarity with the trails cris-crossing the forest had enabled them to circle around to lay the trap. With their engines at a low, quiet idle and no lights showing, all they had to do was wait for the dancing beam of Kismet's head lamp to get a little closer.

The headlight speared up through the darkness like a searchlight as Kismet reached the crest of the hill and unknowingly entered the kill zone. He was just starting to accelerate when Capri let out a shriek. He felt her hands clutching fiercely at his waist, but then she was gone, yanked backward off the Enduro's seat. Without thinking, he laid the bike on its side and rolled clear of its uncontrolled slide, just in time to see--barely visible in the impenetrable night--the last of the Dobermans closing on Capri; one of them was already menacing her, with jaws locked around her forearm. It was in that instant that the gunmen sprang their trap.

In a curious sort of serendipity, the attack of the silently trailing dog pack had stymied the careful planning of the human predators. Their weapons were trained on the place they expected the mounted pair to be, not where the encounter with the canines had placed them. When the guns thundered from out of the trees, the bullets came nowhere near Kismet and Capri.

The kukri flashed twice and the Doberman savaging Capri's arm released its victim in order to emit a tortured howl. Deprived of its forelegs, the wounded animal writhed away in a panic, but its brethren were quick to move in. Kismet grabbed Capri's hand, and slashed his way back toward the edge of the ravine, even as the two gunmen began to shift fire in their direction. A second Doberman went down, decapitated with a single swipe from the kukri, and then they were gone, tumbling down the steep embankment.

Kismet knew they were a long way from being, both literally and figuratively, out of the woods, but when their downhill plummet ended in a tangle of bruise limbs, he risked a hasty question. "Are you all right?"

"No," she replied, gritting her teeth against the pain. "But I guess I'll have to manage."

No sooner had she spoken than the sharp yelps of the remaining Dobermans, still doggedly chasing them, came rolling down the hill. A moment later, the roar of two separate engines drowned out the barking.

One thing at a time, thought Kismet, as he got in front of Capri and brandished the knife.

He met the canine charge with a swing of his kukri. The broad blade sliced into the skull of the foremost attacker, but as the mortally wounded beast scrambled violently away, the blood-slicked haft of the Nepalese fighting knife was wrestled from Kismet's grip. The last remaining Doberman launched at his throat an instant later.

He instinctively blocked with his forearm and felt the animal's powerful jaws close like a vise, the needle sharp teeth sinking to the bone. The momentum of its charge bowled him over. With his free hand, he clawed blindly, searching for the dog's eyes and ears, but found only its slippery coat.

High above, the ATVs crested the hill and began the headlong descent, illuminating the battle between man and beast with their headlights. The two riders veered in opposite directions, an obvious flanking maneuver against which Kismet had no defense; his hands were full anyway.

The dog's teeth were savaging the flesh of his forearm, and no amount of punishment could persuade the animal to release its hold. Fiery agony spread from his fingertips to his elbow and only the narcotic effect of adrenaline kept him from taking refuge in unconsciousness. He was dimly aware of Capri, pounding her fists impotently against the dog's torso, unwittingly exacerbating the injury to his arm by causing the animal to thrash back and forth. Meanwhile, the Colombians had reached the bottom of the ravine and were closing in like pincers from either side.

With a heave, Kismet rolled over, pinning the twisting canine underneath his body. The abrupt move succeeded in loosening the Doberman's grip on his arm, but that minor respite was incidental to what he had in mind. Reaching back with his left hand, he freed the Glock from its holster and shoved it against the beast's rib cage. Twin explosions thundered beneath him as the weapon discharged. It was a risky shot; at such close range, the pressure of gas escaping the muzzle would do almost as much damage as the projectile, and there was no telling what might happen if the rounds deflected off bone or the hard ground underneath. The Doberman yelped violently, all thought of fighting gone, and squirmed from beneath him. Blood gushed from ragged wounds on either side of its torso, and even though it retreated with almost supernatural haste, its death was imminent.

Kismet did not pause to savor the victory. He rolled over and fired from a prone position, emptying the automatic in the direction of the ATV approaching from the left. Behind the glare of the Bombardier's twin headlights, he could distinguish random sparks and knew the driver was returning fire. When the slide on his pistol blew back for the final time, Kismet grabbed Capri's arm and propelled her away from the point where the off-road vehicles would cross their path. He then stood erect at the exact midpoint between them, as if waiting for the axe to fall.

It was, strangely enough, the safest place he could have chosen. Neither gunman dared fire on him, for fear of shooting his comrade; likewise, if either driver shifted course to run him down, they would risk a head-on collision. It was a classic game of chicken, and Kismet wasn't about to blink.

With less than twenty yards between them, the man Kismet had shot at, and possibly wounded, suddenly veered away from the impact zone. As if reacting to a telepathic signal, the other driver swung the front end of his Bombardier toward Kismet, but the latter was already moving; as soon as the first driver had relented, Kismet had sprinted after him, maintaining his position between the two. When the ATV cruised by, he leaped at the driver and snared the collar of the man's shirt. The Colombian was wrenched off his seat, and he and Kismet went tumbling in a tangle of limbs. The ATV, equipped with a safety tether brake, stopped abruptly to form an impromptu barrier between the two men and the remaining vehicle.

Because he was prepared for the impact, Kismet recovered from the bruising crash faster that his adversary and quickly wrestled control of the man's machine pistol. His foe's struggles were halted when Kismet clubbed him alongside the head with the captured weapon. Just as quickly, he scrambled closer to the abandoned Bombardier and took aim at the remaining assailant. A burst from the Skorpion knocked the rider backward off his mount, and when the ATV stalled a moment later, the night was plunged once more into silence.

Capri came to his side. Her carefully manicured exterior was gone, replaced by a costume of blood and dirt, and her wide-eyed gaze was fixed on the carnage all around. Kismet knelt to retrieve his kukri then took her arm. "Come on."

Disdaining the ATVs, he led her back up the hill to the motorcycle. As they climbed, he made a cursory examination of his wounds, then turned his attention to his companion. Her suit had borne the brunt of the Doberman's furry. Beneath the shredded fabric, her wounds amounted to nothing more than bruises and a few abrasions. Kismet's injuries were a little more severe--there were deep punctures on his forearm that would require medical attention to prevent serious infection--but he had been through worse. The bullet wound to his shoulder was barely a graze, for which he was thankful.

Without the constant threat of pursuit, he was able to pay more attention to the trail, and oriented himself toward the edge of the property. As they closed on the wood line however, the sound of gunfire was once more audible in the distance. He put the bike in neutral and coasted to a stop at the edge of the forest. They found themselves on a short hill overlooking the paved driveway. The battlefield below was surreal in the orange glow of the overhead street lamps.

Turino's limousine had almost escaped the property, but had been forced to stop by an impromptu barricade of two vans that were now parked where the wrought iron gate had stood. One of the cars that Turino's wiseguys had used to storm those gates had careened off the road and slammed into a light post; there was no sign of the other. A trail of bodies--some mafia, some cartel--led from the wrecked vehicles to the gatehouse.

Turino and his two bodyguards were still standing, and as Kismet watched, he saw them exchange fire with the two remaining Colombians. Negron's men, perhaps overconfident in their superior firepower, wasted their ammunition, while their opponents directed their single shots with more care and precision. One of them went down with a gaping hole between his eyes, and his sole remaining comrade scrambled behind the vans.

From their vantage, Kismet and Capri could see both sides of battle. The lone Colombian hugged the corner of the van, obviously looking for help that would never come, while the Don began gesturing decisively, directing one of his men to circle around and take the enemy from the flank. It was a classic infantry assault drill, and as that one man headed for the trees, Turino and the other bodyguard began a steady barrage of gunfire to keep their foe pinned down.

"This will be over soon," observed Kismet, speaking over his shoulder. If Capri was troubled by watching her grandfather in a life and death struggle, she gave no indication.

Then something changed.

It felt as if all light and warmth had suddenly drained out of the world, or at least everything in close proximity to the gun battle. Kismet suddenly felt very heavy, and for some reason, no matter how he directed his eyes, he found himself looking at a spot just behind the blockade. It was like staring into a black hole in space. There was a crackle like electricity, then Turino's man was flung backward, past the limousine, to crash into the trees beyond.

The two mafiosi gaped at their stricken comrade, but were likewise unable to divert their attention from the dark entity that glided out from behind the vans. It was Negron, and the Judas Rope at his waist was a vortex, devouring the light.

The remaining bodyguard--it was Salvatore, the man who had pulled Kismet off the tracks of the LIRR--raised his revolver and pumped three shots into the dark monk. The bullets plucked at the fabric of his cassock, then exited with scant resistance. Negron appeared unhurt, but he reacted nonetheless, raising his gnarled fingers then swiping down in a clawing motion. A wave of chilled air radiated from the Judas Rope and Sal was blasted backward. Turino stood alone before his nemesis, his pistol pointing impotently at the ground as he waited for the inevitable.

"Do something!"

He knew that Capri was screaming in his ear, but her voice sounded distant, as if they were separated by a wall of ice. At that moment, the last of Negron's minions burst from his hiding place and ran toward the fray. He leveled a burst at the dazed Sal, killing him instantly, then turned his assault rifle toward Turino.

Kismet shook off his paralysis and twisted the throttle. He squeezed the clutch as the front wheel dropped onto the nearly vertical face of the cliff, letting gravity accelerate them faster than the engine could have in such a short distance. The Colombian sensed their approach an instant too late, swinging around to face them as the Enduro's front tire rammed into his leg. The gunmen was thrown back into the limousine, but the impact twisted the wheel and tore the handlebars from Kismet's grasp. The motorcycle went down on its side and the two riders were pitched headlong across the pavement.

Dazed, Kismet struggled to his feet. On the other side of the limousine, Turino knelt before Negron like a penitent as the dark monk proffered his lethal blessing. The Mafia boss' eyes were bulging from a face purple with trapped blood, and his mouth gasped soundlessly for breath. Kismet remembered that feeling, remembered the despair and helplessness suffered by the dark monk's victims. Negron was omnipotent; he had the power of the devil in his hands, and the only thing that could oppose him was something that Kismet did not possess.

Faith. You fight the devil with faith. But I don't believe in....

Then it hit him. He knew exactly how to defeat Negron.

He ducked inside the limousine and emerged from the opposite door directly in front of the dark priest. He thrust the Glock toward the shadow beneath the cowl, where Negron's face ought to have been. "Let him go."

Negron hissed then, astonishingly, let his captive fall. Turino dropped like a felled tree and Kismet did not dare look away from his nemesis to ascertain whether the Don was still alive. The satanic monk then turned the full might of his black gaze on Kismet. Before the latter could squeeze the trigger, Negron disdainfully backhanded the pistol, knocking it from Kismet's hand with a blow that felt like a blast of liquid nitrogen. He stumbled back almost falling, then rebounded off the limousine. Negron raised his arms, as if in supplication, and began murmuring a strange twisted language. It was Latin, spoken backward.

Kismet felt all life and light drain away, sucked into the vortex of the Judas Rope. His hand felt numb, locked it seemed in a manacle of ice. Every move was a struggle, but all he had to do was make two broad gestures.

He reached up to his forehead then brought his hand down to the level of his waist in a vertical swipe. He then moved his hand up halfway, reached left and moved horizontally. It was the sign of the Cross.

Negron's rumbling invocation faltered.

Kismet then brought out the object he had been concealing behind his back in his left hand. It was a bottle filled with clear liquid. Before the dark monk could move, Kismet began splashing the contents onto his cassock.

"*With blessed water I anoint thee,*" he said in halting Latin. "*In the name of the Father, the Son and the Holy Ghost I baptize thee, and cleanse thee. Your sins are forgiven.*"

A pinprick of light pierced Negron's shadowy countenance as realization dawned; realization of his sins and his defiance of the Almighty entity he had once been wholly devoted to. That tiny fracture, like a hairline crack in a dam, was all it took.

Negron's power fell away in streaks, as if the water of his baptism was literally washing him clean of the evil that had corrupted him for more than a century. His face, hollow and ancient was revealed beneath the cowl and Kismet saw only the pleading visage of a rheumy old man.

It was the curse of Judas. Just as the original betrayer had sought to redeem himself with the sacrifice of his own life, only to be thwarted by an act of chance and eternally damned, so too his modern acolyte, faced with the possibility of his own redemption, had been deserted by his dark master at the moment of his greatest need. As the dark force that sustained him fled away, the burden of his unnaturally long life settled upon his flesh.

Negron bent double, as if an unseen hand was folding him over, and then he crumpled onto the pavement. He managed to raise his eyes heavenward, pleading for mercy from his original lord and master, but his orbs had already turned to dust in their sockets.

Kismet caught a last glimpse of his skeletal grimace, then the cassock deflated into a shapeless mass.

Kismet sagged against the limousine for a moment, feeling as if Negron's demise had taken part of his own soul along in the process, but then pulled himself erect and hastened to Turino's side.

The old capo was still conscious. "Where the devil did you get holy water?"

"From your bar." Kismet turned the bottle to display the Evian label.

"I don't understand. If it wasn't really blessed, how did it stop him?"

"He believed it was. His faith in relics and miracles is what gave him his power, but it was also his Achilles' Heel. His absolute belief in the power of God was stronger than his desire to serve the other side."

Turino laughed again, but was overcome with a coughing fit. Blood streamed from between his lips. Though bruised and battered, Capri hastened to his side, but he shook his head. "Too late for me. You two get out of here before the police come. No need for this to ruin your life."

"No!" Panic seized Capri. Though her relationship with the old man had been troubled, he was her last living blood relative. "We can get you to a hospital. There's time."

The last statement seemed more a question, and her gaze jumped to Kismet, pleading for him to agree, but he knew better. Crimson had already soaked the front of Turino's shirt beneath his jacket, and a dark pool was spreading around him. A bullet had pierced him through the left lung near the heart, possible nicking a vein, and his chest cavity was filling up with fluid. It was only a question of whether he would bleed to death or drown in his own blood. He shook his head imperceptibly, then looked Turino in the eye. "You're Prometheus, aren't you?"

"You think I made it this far in life on my good looks?" Another scarlet-tinged chuckle.

"You were the one who called Capri and told her to contact me. Why?"

"I knew you could protect her."

"What makes me so damned special?" Kismet felt his fingers tightening on the dying man's arm. "Why can't you just trust people with the truth? What is Prometheus? What do you want with me?"

"That is one oath I will not break." A wry smile crossed Turino's bloody lips. "Take care of her Nick. Promise a dying man."

There was nothing he could do to change the old man's mind about revealing his most treasured secret, no effective method of coercing someone who could measure the rest of his life in seconds. "You have my word."

"One more thing," he croaked. The spark of his life force was almost visibly guttering. "A benediction."

Kismet winced. "I'm no priest."

"Your blessing would mean more to me than any last rites." His voice was now barely audible.

Kismet gripped his shoulder. "Godspeed, my friend." Strangely, even though he himself was not a believer, he found the words deeply profound, as if he had somehow tapped into the other man's faith.

"Friend," Turino echoed. "Get her out of here, Nick..."

A few more words took shape on his lips, but there was no breath to give them weight. The old man seemed to melt out of Kismet's grasp. He closed Turino's sightless eyes, and then rose and tugged gently on Capri's arm. "He's right. We have to leave."

Capri's face was a mask of grief, but her eyes held a hint of comprehension, as if in her heart, she knew that such a destiny was inevitable for a man like her grandfather--a man of violence. Perhaps for him it was a better fate than surrendering to the ravages of old age or prolonged illness. She yielded to Kismet's efforts and permitted herself to be drawn along.

Kismet took a step and felt something under his foot. It was the Judas Rope. He looked down at the cord of black hemp, wrapped around the formless cassock. There was no trace of Negron; not even dust. He hugged Capri close then guided her toward the motorcycle.

"Shouldn't we do something about it?" Her voice cracked with lingering grief, but her meaning was clear. "You saw what he did. It's evil. It has to be destroyed."

Kismet shook his head. "That's what he believed and that's why he could do what he did. But it's not really evil. Evil is in men. That's just an old piece of rope. It doesn't mean anything."

Her expression was doubtful but she offered no argument as she climbed on behind him and wrapped her arm around his waist. The Enduro started on the first try and after revving the throttle, Kismet steered toward the highway and sped off into the night.

Later, as the first rays of the rising sun crept across the gray waters of the Atlantic ocean and seeped through the curtain of pine boughs, golden light illuminated the Judas Rope and the hemp fibers began to wither like a piece of fruit fallen from the vine. When the police eventually arrived, all that remained was a twist of ash that quickly crumbled and blew away in the wind. No one even noticed.

END

Enjoy this excerpt from *The Shroud of Heaven*

THE CHAINS OF GOD
January 1991

The Chinook abruptly lurched, gaining fifteen meters of altitude in a heartbeat, only to plunge back down an instant later. The pilot, an insectoid-looking figure in his bulbous headgear and night vision goggles, tilted his head sideways as if to grin at the helpless passengers clinging to nylon web straps in the rear of the helicopter.

"Sorry, mates. Telephone lines."

Nick Kismet nodded indifferently, though his stomach was still pitching from the sudden maneuver. Some of the Gurkhas were not as adept at hiding their momentary nausea; the one he knew only as Sergeant Higgins looked positively green despite the liberal coating of camouflage paint that concealed his face. Of course, in the monochrome display of the PV-7 night vision device affixed to his Kevlar helmet, everything looked green.

The swooping flight of the CH47 seemed an appropriate metaphor for Kismet's life recently. Still trying to overcome the temporary shock of the mobilization orders—a not entirely unexpected event given the escalation of tensions on the Arabian peninsula—he had been further thrown off guard by the strange mission thrust upon him less than a week after his arrival at CENTCOM in Riyadh. Unable to adequately process all of that information, he elected to simply ride it out until things made a little more sense. It was the same philosophy that would, he hoped, get him through this roller coaster insertion.

The flight was probably routine for the pilots. Kismet knew that American Special Forces and British SAS soldiers had already been dropped into enemy-held territory to gather information. As an officer in the US Army Department of Intelligence, albeit a lowly Second Lieutenant and a reservist at that, he was aware of the covert missions that were laying the foundation for the impending assault designed to drive the fourth largest army in the world from their entrenchments in Kuwait. That he would find himself a part of such an operation, much less one that would penetrate deep beyond Iraq's border, was a scenario too ludicrous to even consider. Nevertheless, here he was.

The sergeant swallowed queasily and flashed him an insincere thumbs up. Kismet nodded again.

The Gurkhas signified yet another indecipherable factor in the clandestine mission. He did not know a great deal about the men or their combat division; it was his understanding that they were a sort of foreign legion for the British, originating in Nepal and modeled after the fierce warrior tribe that was their namesake. They were indeed a cosmopolitan bunch, evincing a full spectrum of racial characteristics. Higgins, one of two Caucasian soldiers in the squad, was a Kiwi—originally a citizen of New Zealand.

Though their sand-colored uniforms had been sterilized—no indication of nationality, unit or rank—he had recognized them by virtue of their *kukri* knives. The large chopping knife with a broad, boomerang-shaped blade was their signature weapon. According to their tradition, each recruit was initiated into the elite corps through a bloody ritual in which he was required to behead a young bullock with a single stroke of his *kukri*. A few bits of presumably outdated trivia, however, represented the full extent of Kismet's knowledge about the Gurkhas. *Not much intelligence for an intelligence officer*, he thought sourly.

The presence of soldiers of the United Kingdom of Great Britain was a riddle at least partially explained. According to his commanding officer, the information leading to the mission had been channeled through British resources, and despite the fact that

Kismet, an American officer, had been singled out for special attention, the British would continue to manage the particulars of the insertion. But that did not satisfactorily explain CENTCOM's decision to send this particular unit.

Though legendary for their fierceness, the Gurkha warriors were not an ideal choice for covert insertions. Those assignments, at least where Her Majesty's armed forces were concerned, typically went to the men of the SAS—Special Air Service—who trained extensively for everything from anti-terrorism to hostage rescue to long-range reconnaissance. He could think of only one compelling reason for the commander in charge of the mission to choose men who were not natural citizens of the British commonwealth, but rather rogues and expatriates: They were expendable. Kismet wondered if he fell into that category as well.

What little he had been told had not inspired him to confidence in the success, much less the importance, of their mission. He knew only that it involved the possible defection of a high-value target; someone who might be a member of Saddam Hussein's inner circle of advisors. After reading the operation order, a bare bones overview of what he would be expected to accomplish, Kismet had immediately become suspicious. His first impulse was that the supposed defection was an elaborate ruse designed to test the capabilities of coalition forces in penetrating Iraqi air defenses. Despite assurances otherwise, he remained skeptical.

The Chinook continued through the desert night, following the nap of the earth to avoid detection by radar, jinking and swooping when necessary to dodge phone lines and possible SAM sites. There was little for the passengers to see through the small portals on either side of the ungainly looking aircraft. Even with the aid of night vision goggles, the desert was a featureless wasteland. Each *wadi*—the dry gullies that cut randomly across the dunes—looked very much like the next, but one of them concealed the man he had been sent to meet.

In the earpiece of his headset, Kismet heard the pilots continue their exchange of information, calling out the obstacles that lay in their path as they became visible. He knew they were nearing their destination because the co-pilot regularly updated their ETA. The countdown was now a matter of mere minutes.

"City lights," observed the flight officer, pointing over the pilot's shoulder. He consulted a military map specifically designed for use with night vision gear. "That's Nasiriyah."

"Close as I want to get."

"I have a visual of the target," the co-pilot announced. His voice dropped to an incredulous murmur. "Bloody wanker's having a fag."

Kismet absent-mindedly translated the idiomatic expression. Somewhere out in the desert, the man they were supposed to meet was smoking a cigarette. In the display of the night vision devices used by the flight crew, the pencil-thin ember would flash beacon bright as the man drew smoke into his lungs, even from a distance of several hundred meters.

One of the Gurkhas tisked. "He should know better. Must be an officer."

Kismet laughed, grateful for their humor. He was the highest ranked person onboard and well aware of the age-old rivalry between enlisted men and officers, but he took no offense at the veiled jab. This close to the objective, with his adrenaline spiking, he needed the distraction. Nervously, he checked his gear one last time.

The mission called for the team to be dropped near a rendezvous point established by the Iraqi defector. This would give them an opportunity to reconnoiter the area, just in case it was a trap. The Gurkhas would then dig in, securing a temporary forward operating base, while Kismet made contact with the defector. They expected their mission to last no more than forty-eight hours, but even that short time span required each man to carry several liters of drinking water, along with all of their combat gear and body armor. In addition to his ruck, Kismet carried a stubby CAR15, the carbine version of the M16A2 assault rifle, and his personal side arm, a Beretta M9 automatic pistol. Most of the Gurkhas carried American M203s—M16s equipped with integrated 40 millimeter grenade launchers under the rifle barrel—but two of the men were packing fully automatic Minimi light machine guns. Kismet noted that the latter pair would not be carrying their own water, a fair trade for the additional weight of a thousand rounds of ammunition apiece, stored in drum magazines and cloth bandoliers. Ideally, they would not have to expend a single round. If everything went according to plan, they would be returning to Saudi airspace with only their water supply depleted.

The Chinook dropped quickly to the desert floor,

bouncing the passengers violently one final time. The Gurkhas immediately burst into action, pitching canvas bags out into the sand as the aft ramp slowly descended. Their movements seemed practiced, belying the tension that Kismet knew each man must be silently enduring. After swiftly disembarking, the small group of soldiers huddled close to the ground as the twin rotors of the Chinook whipped up a sandstorm. A few heartbeats later, the helicopter vanished into the night.

Higgins removed his NOD and gazed skyward, fixing the North Star with a fingertip. He extended his other arm at a ninety-degree angle. "Our guy's that way. Wong, Renke, dig us a nice little den. Lieutenant, I guess you're leading the way."

Kismet was thrown by the Kiwi sergeant's pronunciation—"Lef-tenant"—and gaped dumbly at the other man for several awkward seconds. "Sorry," he finally mumbled, hefting the CAR15 and turning in the direction Higgins had indicated. "Let's go."

They stayed low to the ground, pausing at the dune crests to survey the landscape for signs of the enemy. Visual contact with the defector—still puffing away on his cigarette, or perhaps chain-smoking one after another—was reestablished almost immediately. They were less than two hundred meters from the man's location.

"I don't see anyone else," Kismet murmured. "No vehicles either."

"How the hell did he get out here?" Higgins wondered aloud. "Flying bloody carpet?"

Kismet stifled a chuckle. "Maybe." He turned to the sergeant. "I guess this is it. I'm counting on you guys to watch my back."

The Gurkha nodded, but Kismet was not

overwhelmed with confidence. Nevertheless he crept forward, topped the dune and scooted down the other side, moving unaccompanied toward the sole Iraqi. If it was a trap, he alone would face that peril. Even if the Gurkhas brought their firepower to bear, there was little hope of his surviving the first moments of a hostile encounter.

As he drew closer, he was able to make out the facial features of the defector. The bland countenance seemed pale beneath his thick black brow, as if the man had somehow managed to avoid direct exposure to the sun during his life on the cusp of the Arabian desert.

Only the nervous quivering of the cigarette at his lips bore testimony that his bloodless hue had more to do with anxiety than pigmentation. In the green-tinted display of his night optics, Kismet noted that the man's pupils were tiny white dots. The incessant lighting and smoking of cigarettes had compromised the waiting defector's ability to see naturally in the dark, verifying the earlier observation made by the Chinook pilot. Either the man was too inexperienced in matters of survival to know better, or he simply didn't care.

Kismet paused, scanning the surrounding desert for any indication of an ambush party in concealment.

Nothing. If the defector was bait for a trap, then it was a well covered snare. He edged forward, circling around the smoking man, and approached from his left side. When no more than ten meters separated them, he rose from his cautious crawl and pushed his goggles out of the way.

There was no way to avoid startling the oblivious defector, but he tried to minimize the shock by softly clearing his throat. The Iraqi man turned his head slowly, almost absent-mindedly, before reacting exactly as Kismet feared he would. Yet, as the man flailed backwards, waving his hands defensively, Kismet's apprehension that he had walked into a trap eased considerably. The defector had not groped for a concealed weapon or called out in alarm; no hidden accomplices had leapt to the man's aid. Kismet waited motionless for his contact to recover.

"*Is salaam aleekum.*" *Peace be upon you.*

The softly spoken greeting did not seem to soothe the frightened man, but he heard the muttered, traditional reply: "*Wa aleekum issalaam.*" *And upon you be peace.*

"Well that's a good sign," Kismet muttered in English. His grasp of Arabic was not as strong as he would have liked. A lifetime of world travel with his father had immersed him repeatedly in foreign language environments, but he considered himself fluent only in the Romance languages.

However, despite the fact that his self-directed words were barely audible, the defector suddenly brightened. "You are Mr. Kismet?" he asked in halting English.

Kismet blinked. In his pre-mission briefing, he had been given precious little information about how the rendezvous would proceed. There had been no arrangement made for passwords and countersigns. His commander was unable even to supply a name for the defector, much less any sort of safeguarding procedures. The last thing he had anticipated was for the Iraqi man to know his name. He switched off his night vision goggles and swung them up, away from his face. "That's right."

"*Il-Hamdulillaah,*" breathed the man. "God be praised. I feared that you would not be coming. I am Samir Al-Azir."

He sensed that the man expected to be recognized,

but the name triggered no memories. He smiled and gave the man a knowing nod, hoping nothing would happen to further expose his ignorance. "We should probably get moving."

Samir seemed further relieved at the suggestion, as if suddenly remembering why he was lurking in the cold desert night. He flipped his cigarette onto the sand. "Yes, yes. Follow me."

Before he could protest, Samir turned and began climbing the dune. Dumbly, Kismet started after the Iraqi. At the top of the rise, he signaled the waiting Gurkhas by extending his arms out to either side, as though waiting to be searched. The unusual gesture was a previously established signal, indicating to his comrades that he was not being taken along under duress. If Samir noticed, he said nothing.

Based on his recollection of aerial reconnaissance photographs of the area, Kismet knew that the nearest road was more than a kilometer from their present location. That roadway was a featureless track snaking across the desert to provide access to the semi-permanent Bedouin communities, and more importantly, to expedite the deployment of troops in the event of a war. With that war now looming large, the likelihood of armed forces moving along the highway was greatly increased. He did not find Samir's eagerness to approach that destination encouraging, but what he saw as they crested yet another dune a few moments later increased his anxiety tenfold. Barely visible across the intervening distance was the unmistakable silhouette of a vehicle waiting beside the highway.

It took another ten minutes of struggling over the uneven terrain to reach the parked sedan, long enough for him to ascertain that the battered, silver Mercedes was unoccupied. "Where are we going, Samir?"

The defector flashed a grin over his shoulder, but Kismet could see the other man's concern etched in deep lines across his forehead. "Not far. The tell is nearby."

Tell? There were many ways of interpreting the word, none of which made sense in the context. He frowned, but did not press for more information. Instead, he opened the rear driver side door of the sedan and carefully slipped inside. Samir's pale face registered confusion at Kismet's decision to sit behind instead of beside him, but he said nothing as he turned the key and eased the car onto the paved road.

Kismet rested the CAR15 on the seat beside him, shifting the waist pack of his load-bearing vest to avoid sitting on it. That the Army-issue equipment had not been designed for use in the cramped interior of a passenger vehicle was only one factor owing to his choice of the rear seat. Sitting in the back represented an attempt, however insignificant, to take a measure of control over the situation. He was completely at Samir's mercy. Even if the defector meant him no harm, there would be no effective way for Kismet to respond in the event of a sudden crisis. From the back seat at least, should the worst case scenario play out, he would be able to encourage the Iraqi to heed his suggestions by holding the business end of his sidearm to the base of the other man's skull.

True to his word, Samir drove the car only a few kilometers along the highway before once more pulling off into the sand. Kismet hastened from the confining interior of the sedan, and began scanning the dunes for any sign of enemy forces. They appeared to be alone in the night. Samir lit another cigarette then motioned for Kismet to follow as he headed into the desert.

The path chosen by the Iraqi defector led north across a section of flat land where bare rock struggled up through the ubiquitous layer of sand. Kismet gradually became aware that they were descending into a low valley sculpted by centuries of wind and, perhaps in a forgotten age, water. In the otherworldly green display of his goggles, he saw clear evidence of previous foot traffic along their course; not simply a scattering of prints, but a line of disruption indicating the passage of several people. He hefted the CAR15, his thumb poised on the fire selector and his finger on the outside of the trigger guard, but resisted the impulse to spin strategies for dealing with a hostile encounter. He would likely be outnumbered and outgunned in such a situation, so there was little to be gained by worrying. Samir, however, seemed to relax, as if each step brought him closer to a place of refuge. Their destination soon became apparent.

From the outside, it did not look like a cave, merely a bruise in the surface of a vertical rock face which might simply have been the product of an ancient boulder collision. Only on closer inspection could Kismet perceive the depth of the cut in the rock and the fact that the stone surface was not stone at all, but weathered bricks of baked clay laid one atop another. It was not a cave, but a structure built by men in the middle of the desert and almost completely hidden beneath the dunes. Samir ducked through the narrow slit without hesitation. An almost blinding flare in the midst of Kismet's night vision display indicated a light source within. He switched the goggles off and swiveled them out of the way, then crouched down and followed blindly.

The passage beyond was narrow. His shoulders scraped against brick on either side as he descended along a crumbling staircase. The steps, like the structure itself, were clearly the work of human artifice, but their condition suggested centuries of both use and neglect. They were in an ancient place.

At the foot of the stairwell, he saw the source of the light. As his guide stepped forward into a large antechamber, he could clearly make out the flickering of several randomly placed oil lamps. It was not until he moved out from the narrow recess, however, that Kismet realized they were not alone.

Before he could bring his carbine up, or even identify a target, Samir hastened in front of him, arms extended. "No, no, Mr. Kismet. This is my family."

Kismet exhaled sharply and lowered the weapon. In the undulating lamp-light he made out several human shapes: an elegantly dressed woman, her head covered by a colorful scarf; a teenage boy who seemed a younger, thinner version of Samir; and several more indistinguishable lumps, hidden beneath blankets on the floor. In all, there appeared to be a dozen people camped out in the hidden structure, possibly representing three generations of Samir's clan.

"Family," echoed Kismet, the significance of the revelation sinking in. "No one said anything about your family."

Samir looked shocked. "I could not leave them. When it is learned what I have done, they would be made to suffer. Such is the way with President Hussein."

Kismet felt a moment of self-loathing for having questioned the matter. "That's not what I meant. It's just…well, we didn't develop a contingency for exfiltrating more than one person. There won't be room on the helo for all of us."

Samir's expression fell, prompting Kismet to

hastily augment his statement. "What I mean is, we'll have to make some changes to the plan."

The Iraqi seemed pleased at the promise and brightened once more. "Allah is great."

"Yeah," muttered Kismet, loosening the chin strap on his helmet as he surveyed the room a second time. "Say, you didn't all come here in that one car?"

Samir grinned. "No. There is also a truck."

"Any more surprises?"

"No more surprises." His voice dropped to a conspiratorial whisper. "Do you wish to see it?"

Kismet sensed the defector was no longer talking about the truck, and that whatever he was referring to would indeed be a surprise, but the only way to know for certain was to play along.

"Sure."

Samir launched into motion again, but did not move toward the stairwell as Kismet expected. Instead, he crossed the antechamber, picked up one of the lamps, and headed toward an arched entryway on the opposite side.

"The truck is here? Inside this—whatever it is?"

"These are the ruins of Tall al Muqayyar. We are very near to what you in the West call Ur of the Chaldees. It was the birthplace of Ibraiim; Abraham, the father of Ismail. Our nation takes its name from this place: Uruk. It is the birthplace of civilization."

"You don't say." He thought Samir sounded like a tour guide. He had studied enough source material about Iraq to recognize the truth of Samir's words, but ancient ruins held little appeal; he preferred the company of the living. "We are under the ground though?"

"The sands come and go. The ruins have been excavated several times since their discovery almost two centuries ago, but the sand always returns. In this instance, I have used the sand to conceal the main entrance to the ruin." He gestured with the lamp, throwing a wavering yellow glow into the shroud of darkness. Beyond the antechamber was a larger room, its ultimate width and breadth beyond the scope of Kismet's unaided eyesight. He resisted the impulse to swivel the goggles down, electing instead to wait for

Samir's lamp to expose the room's secrets. As the Iraqi strode purposefully forward, his light cut a swath through the darkness in the middle of the chamber. After only a few steps, the bare floor disappeared beneath an increasingly dense accumulation of desert sand.

The lamp's rays soon revealed a vehicle in the buried chamber—what looked to Kismet like a deuce and a half, or 2.5-ton truck—its rear cargo area covered by a low slung canvas tarpaulin. The truck appeared to be a cast-off military vehicle, broken, repaired and mongrelized to the extent that its origins were unrecognizable. Beyond the truck, the sand rose up in a vast dune, completely blocking what must have served as the main entrance to the ruin. Samir placed his lamp on the rear bumper of the truck, but hesitated there.

Kismet tried to peer into the tent-like enclosure, but saw nothing in the shadows. "Well?"

"Forgive me. I am a coward. President Hussein says it is not thehand of Allah—that it is a Zionist trick—but he does not touch it. No sane man dares touch it."

"The hand of Allah?" Again Kismet sensed that he was expected to know more than he did. He decided to end the charade. "I'm sorry, Samir, but I have no clue what you're talking about. I've never heard of you and I haven't the faintest idea why you think I'd care about what's in that truck."

His declaration hit Samir like a blow. The Iraqi staggered back, his hands moving nervously. "You-you are not Kismet."

"I am Nick Kismet. Pretty sure I'm the only one." Given the unique circumstances surrounding the choosing of his name, he felt safe in the assertion.

"But then you must know. You of all people would know…" Kismet shrugged. "They didn't tell me much about the mission, Samir. I didn't even know that you were the person I'd be meeting."

He could tell the revelation troubled Samir, but the Iraqi began nodding slowly, as if to clear his head. "I believe I understand. When you have seen it, everything will become clear."

Kismet stared once more into the cargo area of the truck. His thoughts began to spin out of control. Just what was the secret Samir was delivering to him? *The hand of Allah?* Had the defector snatched one of Saddam's much-rumored nuclear weapons? Almost trembling with eagerness, Kismet laid the CAR15 on the deck and pulled himself into the truck.

He had to crouch down under the low hanging tarpaulin, but once inside, his ability to see in the darkness began to improve. He could discern that the cargo bay was empty save for a lone object in the center, secured to a wooden pallet by a single nylon rope that zigzagged back and forth across the bed of the vehicle. Whatever lay beneath that web was further concealed by a heavy blanket of dark material, but he could make out a vaguely familiar silhouette. It didn't look like any kind of nuclear warhead.

Samir held his light close to the opening. "I would advise you not to touch it, but of course, you would know more about this than I."

Kismet stared in disbelief at the veiled bundle. He recognized the outline of the object only because it looked exactly the way it had in a motion picture he had enjoyed countless times as a child. "What the…is this some kind of joke?"

Samir's eyes seemed to dance eagerly in the flicker of lamplight. "Does this not buy freedom for my family and I?"

Kismet spun to face the Iraqi. "If this really is what you want me to believe it is, then how in hell did you get it?"

"President Hussein has long feared that if the Zionists—the Israelis—learned that we possessed it, they would not hesitate to use any means necessary to take it back. And once they possessed it, they would be emboldened to make war with all Arabs. Yet he hesitated to destroy it—what if it truly is the work of Allah? But now with America ready to invade, he can wait no longer. If it is from Allah, then Allah must decide how to save it, or so President Hussein says. He ordered me to have it destroyed. Of course I was supervised, but I managed to switch it with a decoy. It was very costly. I had to find enough gold to fool the others, but I did. And when the chance arose, I sent for you."

Sent for me? He blinked furiously, trying to process what Samir was telling him. "Hold it a second." He gestured emphatically at the object. "What I meant was, how did this end up in Iraq? I thought it was in Ethiopia. Or Egypt." *Or some US Army warehouse*, he didn't add.

Samir pondered for a moment, then laughed. He shook his head. "None of those rumors are true. When those who ruled this land before—the Babylonians—sacked Jerusalem two thousand six hundred years ago, they took as spoil all the treasures of the Jews. This also was captured, but King Nebuchadnezzar wisely spread the rumor that it had been taken away by Jewish refugees before their temple fell. As the holiest of the Jewish treasures, it was a trophy of victory over God himself, and the Babylonians hid it in the deepest part of the Esagila—the temple of Marduk. When the Jews returned to their land after the Persian Empire conquered the Babylonians, it never occurred to them to ask for it back. They did not know it was there, and in time, it was forgotten by all.

"Even the first archaeologists to excavate the temple did not find the secret chamber where it lay, but when President Hussein decided to rebuild the glory of Babylon, his engineers—and I was part of that group—did find it."

Kismet shook his head incredulously, his mind racing. Samir had requested him personally. How had the defector learned about him? And why had the Iraqi believed he would know, or even care, about some three-thousand-year-old relic? He rubbed the bridge of his nose, trying to banish the rampant speculations in order to form a strategy. "All right, this complicates things further. If we're going to get this out—" he gestured at the covered artifact, "—and everyone else, then we're going to need at least three helos and probably a shitload of close air support." He looked thoughtfully at the truck. "Either that or drive out. Think we could make it to Syria in this?"

Samir frowned. "You would risk bringing it so close to Zionist forces? Their agents would know of it the moment we crossed the border. I would think you, of all people, would want to conceal this from the Israelis."

Once again, Kismet got the feeling that Samir was dialed into some secret and erroneous source of information about him. He decided it was time to disabuse the Iraqi of those notions. Twisting around on the flatbed deck, he hopped backward onto the sand covered floor to stand face to face with the other man. "Listen, Samir. My orders are to get you out—you. I am willing to risk my life to carry out those orders. I am willing to risk my life to help your family as well. But I am not about to put my life on the line for a… For some movie prop. If you insist on trying to get that thing back to friendly turf, then we are going to use the safest possible route, and if that means we drive through downtown Tel Aviv, well then I just don't give a shit."

Samir gaped in disbelief, but before he could even begin to frame a reply, a faint hissing sound distracted both men. Kismet turned toward the source of the noise and saw sand sliding down the face of the dune wall. His reaction was late by a fraction of a second.

He reached for the CAR15, but it was not where he expected, depending from its sling on his shoulder. Suddenly, the sand barrier erupted in a flurry of bodies and movement. Human shapes burst from the dune wall like reanimated corpses summoned from their graves. Remembering that his carbine lay on the deck of the truck, Kismet reached instead for the M9 holstered on his hip, but there was no time. One of the figures reared up before him and something hard and heavy crashed into his jaw. As he staggered back, the sound of Samir's cries of alarm dissolved into a ringing noise that seemed to originate inside his skull. Hands swarmed over him, stripping away his pistol and restraining his arms. He hovered at the edge of consciousness, vaguely aware that his wrists were being pressed together behind his back, secured with a hard plastic zip-tie.

He struggled both against the shackles that bound his hands and the darkness that was overwhelming him, but in the end both battles were in vain.

* * *

Kismet awoke with a start, reflexively trying to raise his hands to shield himself from the object that filled his blurry gaze; someone had peeled back his right eyelid and was tapping the sclera of that eye with a fingertip. His hands did not respond, still securely bound behind his back, but the ferocity of his reaction was enough to remove him from the immediate threat.

He now saw the instigator of his torment, a lean lupine individual wearing desert battle dress fatigues similar to his own. The man's Caucasian features and dishwater blond hair suggested that he was a Westerner, but Kismet did not get the impression that his antagonist was there in order to rescue him. The man flashed a humorless smile, then turned to one of his comrades. The words he spoke sounded familiar, but Kismet didn't recognize the language. It might have been Hebrew, but with his head still swimming from the assault, he couldn't be sure.

The wolfish man leaned close again, thrusting something against his jaw. The object was frigid but yielding—an instant cold compress. "I told him he is lucky he didn't kill you," the man volunteered in English.

Kismet couldn't fathom why. He thought about Samir's words. "Israelis?" he croaked.

The man chuckled, again without a trace of humor. "Do you think you can stand?"

"Not without help," he replied, honestly.

Grasping the front straps of Kismet's combat harness, the man shifted his weight backward, lifting him from his supine position. Pain radiated from Kismet's bruised jaw and stabbed through his head. Bright sparks of light swam in his field of vision and for a moment, Kismet feared he would lose consciousness again. The man continued to hold him erect as his legs buckled, his head swooning, until the fog gradually receded. The ice pack slipped away from his cheek, but remained tucked in the space between his neck and the stiff collar of his flak jacket.

He saw that he was once more in the antechamber where he had first encountered Samir's family. They were all there, including the defector himself, lined up against one wall of the room in a classic hostage pose: kneeling with fingers laced together behind their heads. Some of them, mostly the children, were weeping and ululating. Half a dozen men in desert-pattern uniforms were spread throughout the room, each wielding a small submachine gun.

Kismet easily recognized their arsenal: Heckler & Koch MP5Ks, the first choice of hostage rescue and commando teams worldwide. Unlike the man who held his load straps however, the rest of the combat force wore camouflage mesh screens over their heads, obscuring their faces, and soft boonie hats that matched their fatigues. One of the men also had Kismet's carbine slung over a shoulder.

He returned his gaze to the man before him. "You didn't answer my question."

His captor, judging that Kismet now stood on his own, relaxed his grip on the LBE straps. He maintained his silence a moment longer, reaching out to grasp the hilt of the Ka-Bar knife which hung from an inverted sheath on the front of Kismet's harness. As he drew the blade, Kismet shifted his eyes downward, surreptitiously checking the rest of his equipment. He immediately saw that, in addition to the knife, his other defensive weapon, the M9 Beretta pistol, had been removed from its holster. There was no sign of his helmet or night vision goggles, but every other piece of gear he carried seemed to have been left alone.

"Since I have no doubt that you and I will eventually meet again, and since it will not benefit you in any way, I will give you my name." He spoke with a faint accent that Kismet couldn't pin down.

The man circled behind him, deftly cutting through the zip-tie with the razor-sharp combat blade. As Kismet's hands broke free, the man resumed talking. "I am Ulrich Hauser. And lest you take the wrong impression, I am not a member of the Bundeswehr, or any other recognized army. I am not, I might add, an Israeli. Be thankful for that."

Kismet did not question why this distinction was important, but took note of it; Samir had made a similar statement. He turned his head, following as Hauser continued his orbit, but resisted the impulse to massage his wrists, letting his hands hang loosely at his hips. "Should I take from your comments that you're not going to kill us?"

Hauser returned to his starting point directly in front of Kismet. He held the Ka-Bar contemplatively between them for a moment, then slipped the naked blade into his own belt. At that instant, for no apparent reason, Kismet felt raw adrenaline dumping into his bloodstream, a premonition of something terrible about to happen, perhaps already beginning.

Hauser took the CAR15 from his accomplice and turned toward the line of hostages. It seemed to

Kismet that he was moving in slow motion, but that was simply a trick of hyper-awareness. He didn't even have time to open his mouth in protest.

The carbine erupted in a spray of fire and noise. Hauser moved it from side to side, hosing Samir and his family with an unceasing torrent of 5.56-millimeter ammunition. Kismet felt hot bile flash into his throat and he involuntarily jerked toward Hauser, hands reaching for the gun even though he knew it was too late. Three of Hauser's men intercepted him, locking their fists around his biceps.

He knew the air must be filled with the screams of the dying but all he could hear was the endless roar of gunfire. A chaotic pattern of gore and pocked brick now decorated the wall of the chamber, a carpet of corpses spread out beneath, yet Hauser did not relent until the last round was fired. Only when the final brass cartridge was ejected, landing with a barely audible tinkling sound in the eerie silence of the aftermath, did Hauser raise the barrel of the weapon.

Kismet's mouth worked, trying to form words, but there was only rage and futility in his throat. Hauser faced him now, his lips drawn back in a fierce grimace, his eyes dancing hungrily. Without warning, he thrust the gun sideways at Kismet, who reflexively caught it, his left hand grabbing the stock while his right fingers wrapped around the shortened barrel of the carbine. He felt the sting of hot metal scorching his skin but did not release the now-impotent weapon.

"Why?" he whispered, finding at least that single word. It seemed inadequate, but it was all he could manage.

Before Hauser could reply, if he intended to at all, a voice called out from the far end of the antechamber where it passed into the main area. The words were in the same unrecognizable language, but the commando leader understood. Nodding, he fired back a quick response in the same tongue, then addressed his sole remaining captive.

"This prize is not for you, Kismet. Not now."

The short declaration was not at all what Kismet was expecting.

"What the hell are you talking about? You did all this for…for that thing?" He gestured toward the main chamber where he had last seen the truck and its mysterious, ancient cargo.

"One day, you will understand what we have done, and why it had to be done." Despite his earlier, almost gleeful reaction to his act of violence, Hauser now seemed more subdued. He turned without another word and began striding toward the exit. His men followed, keeping wary eyes on the one man who did not belong to their number.

Kismet glanced down at the CAR15 in his hands, feeling the throb of pain in his right palm. Blue smoke continued to waft from the barrel and the air was heavy with the smell of burned cordite. He knew without looking that Hauser had shot off every round in the magazine, rendering the weapon temporarily useless, but there was something Hauser either did not know or had forgotten about. In two clip-on pouches, one on either side of his combat belt, Kismet carried spare magazines. He tried to estimate exactly how long it would take him to eject the spent clip, tear open the clasp on the ammo pocket, extract a spare and jam it into the magazine well. Two seconds?

Time enough for the cautious commandos to take preemptive measures; their weapons were already loaded.

As he weighed his options, the last of the men

exited the antechamber, leaving him alone with the dead. He moved toward the passageway, walking slowly enough that he did not alarm the gunmen.

The commandos had made short work of the sand barrier Samir had used to cover the main entrance. The far end of the ruin was exposed to the chilly desert night, illuminated now only by the stars.

Their work finished, the assault team began climbing into the rear of the truck. Hauser lingered behind them, catching his eye once more.

"Do not fear, Kismet. It will be kept safe until the world is ready."

"Safe?" he echoed hollowly. "With you? You're a fucking psychopath."

Hauser hopped onto the rear bumper and pulled himself half inside the truck. He then turned to Kismet and grinned, shifting his head back slightly, like a werewolf ready to howl. Kismet shook his head to clear the image. "Who are you?"

"I've given you my name," Hauser replied, elevating his voice to be heard as the diesel engine rumbled to life. "Anything else I could say would only serve to confuse you. However, this much I will reveal: We are the chains of God, sealing Pandora's box for the preservation of mankind. We are Prometheus, guiding the destiny of the world until humanity is ready to ascend Olympus."

The words sounded like a mantra; a pledge learned by rote. The truck lurched into gear, spinning its wheels for a moment before finding purchase in the loose sand. Hauser steadied himself, then shouted over the din. "Do not try to follow us, Kismet. I have done what I can to spare you, but I will take no responsibility for the fortunes of war."

Something Hauser had said earlier now echoed in

his mind. *I told him he is lucky he didn't kill you.*

"Why?" he shouted as the vehicle moved away from the chamber. "Why didn't you kill me?"

Hauser broke into unrestrained laughter; his first honest display of emotion. "Kismet, if I killed you, your mother would have my head."

If Hauser had anything more to say, it was lost as the truck moved away, threading the narrow alley between brick structures and sand dunes. Kismet took a step after them, then stopped as rage built in his chest and arms.

He pressed the button to eject the spent magazine from the carbine, then slammed a fresh clip into the weapon, slapping it with a mechanically practiced action to guarantee that the first round would not jam. He released the bolt, advancing a cartridge into the firing chamber, then raised it to shoulder height and sighted down the stubby barrel at the receding truck. Even as his finger flexed on the trigger, he knew the shot would be a futile gesture. He might get lucky and actually hit one of the escaping killers, but the odds were not good. With a defeated sigh, he lowered the gun and backed into the now deserted ruins. The oil lamps placed by Samir and his family continued to illuminate the abattoir that was the antechamber.

The sulfur odor of gunpowder lingered in the air, but there was a new scent added to the mix—the unmistakable stench of death. He had been in the presence of the dying and recently passed, but nothing like this. He had never seen healthy, vibrant individuals so violently ripped away from the world. It took a deliberate effort for him to search the memories of his combat skills training in order to determine his next action.

Like an automaton plugged into a new program, he

lurched into action, systematically moving down the row of shattered bodies. The 5.56millimeter green-tip ball ammunition had not ripped their flesh apart as larger and softer lead rounds might. Instead, the bullets had stabbed neat little holes clear through the victims, lacerating intestines and vital organs, wreaking internal damage with less outward trauma than might have been expected.

Samir and the woman Kismet assumed to be his wife had both expired from their wounds, but two of the younger children and one older male still drew ragged breaths. One of the children, a girl, clung to consciousness, whimpering when he turned her over to inspect the wounds. It was enough to throw him out of his almost mechanical routine, and he felt hot tears streaking down his face. He drew out one of two Syrettes of morphine hanging from a breakaway chain around his neck and quickly injected the contents into the girl's thigh. Her agonized moans soon gave way to shallow breathing.

He knew the morphine would probably kill her, but that would merely hasten the inevitable and with less anguish. None of those who still drew breath would survive the night. Perhaps with the care of skilled surgeons in a state of the art trauma center, the hand of the Reaper might be stayed, but here in the desert with only Kismet's basic first-aid skills and even more rudimentary first-aid kit, it was foolish to entertain hope. He cradled her in his arms and waited for the inevitable silence that would follow her final gasp.

"Bloody hell."

The low whisper from behind startled Kismet, but he did not let it show. Instead he turned his head slowly and saw Sergeant Higgins and two of the Gurkhas.

Higgins was standing exactly where Hauser had been at the moment of the massacre, and was surveying both the carnage and the scattering of 5.56 millimeter brass casings on the floor. Higgins was solemn. "Did you do this, sir?"

Unable to find his voice, Kismet shook his head.

Higgins nodded slowly. "That's good enough for me, mate." His words carried the implication that Kismet's denial might not be sufficient for the others who would eventually ask the same question. The Gurkha continued. "We've got to move out, sir. Something has happened. About half an hour ago, the northern sky—by that I mean the sky over Baghdad—lit up like the end of the world. I think it's finally started."

Kismet eased the mortally wounded child to the floor and stood. "How did you get here?"

"We ran, didn't we?" Higgins managed a triumphant grin. "More like walked fast. We followed your tracks to the road. After that, it was trusting luck that we were going the right way and that you hadn't gone too far."

"Luck." Kismet looked around the chamber, at last spying his helmet and night vision goggles. "Let's get moving. We're going to need the devil's own luck to get through this."

They filed back up the staircase with Kismet leading the way. A fourth Gurkha waited at the entrance to the ruin, a guard left behind by Higgins. With a nod to the sergeant, he fell in with the rest as they marched single file back up to the roadway.

In the still desert night, Kismet could make out the sound of a distant vehicle engine, perhaps more than one. It might simply have been the sound of Hauser's captured truck stealing away with the prize, but they couldn't afford to make that assumption. They were deep in enemy territory.

One of the Gurkhas approached Samir's sedan cautiously, peering through the windows. Higgins turned to Kismet. "At least we won't have to walk back."

The soldier tried the door handle.

Do not try to follow...

Kismet threw off his paralysis and started toward the car. "Get away from there..."

The Mercedes suddenly split in two, lifting off the ground in an eruption of orange fire and black smoke. The shock wave slapped Kismet and the others to the ground and sucked the air from their lungs. He felt a heavy weight strike him in the chest—something warm and yielding—and reflexively pushed it away.

It took only a moment or two for the stunned group of soldiers to recover. Higgins, the most senior among the squad, sprang to his feet, sweeping left and right with his weapon. "What the fuck was that?"

The Gurkha sergeant was screaming, but Kismet could barely hear through the ringing in his ears. They had all been close to the blast, but none as close as the soldier who had triggered it.

"Singh!"

Kismet followed the line of Higgins' shocked gaze and saw what was left of Corporal Sanjay Singh of the 6th Queen Elizabeth's Own Gurkha Rifles.

The blast had knocked him away from the detonation site a fraction of a second ahead of the flames. The live ordnance in his equipment vest had been triggered by the shock wave, but his flak jacket had directed the force of those secondary explosions away from his torso. Nevertheless, despite escaping the force of fire, Singh's skeleton had been pulverized within by the release of energy, and his remains were now an almost-shapeless mass of smoking fabric and flesh near Kismet's feet. Kismet saw the streaks of blood on his own BDU blouse and felt his gorge rise a second time.

Another of the Gurkhas, the machine-gunner Private Mutabe, was down, his left arm opened to the bone by a slashing fragment of metal. The fourth soldier knelt beside the wounded African and fished out his Syrette, injecting him with a dose of morphine to dull the pain.

"Jesus Christ," scowled Higgins, stomping closer to where Kismet stood, reeling. "What the fuck was that?"

"Car bomb," murmured Kismet, feeling a fool for stating the obvious. "They booby trapped it. He tried to warn me."

"They? Who the fuck are they?" And then, phrasing it so it sounded like a curse, the sergeant added: "Sir."

"I don't know." Kismet's answer was inaudible.

"Well we're fucked good now, sir." He jerked a thumb at the column of smoke that spilled up into the night sky. "That's going to bring everyone within fifty klicks right down on top of us, and in case you hadn't noticed, we're down to three."

"I noticed," Kismet muttered. He turned away from Singh's corpse, fixing the sergeant in his gaze, scouring his memory for the leadership skills he had been taught but never applied. When he spoke again, it was more forcefully. "I noticed, sergeant. Now get your shit together and let's get moving. Those two can buddy up. You and I will carry Singh."

He felt like a fraud for saying it, for using a command voice; he had never commanded men before. And as he watched Higgins' face quivering with barely contained rage, he wondered if he had made a mistake. Higgins would blame him for this. He was the officer, the mission leader, and responsible for the lives of his subordinates.

An image of Hauser leering like a coyote flashed in his mind. *No*, he decided. *I didn't do this.* Hauser had murdered Samir and his innocent children. Hauser's men had rigged the car to blow.

You and I will eventually meet again…

In that instant, he knew that he would endure. For the sake of revenge, if nothing else, he would survive.

Perhaps Higgins saw that light of resolve igniting in Kismet's eyes. Or maybe it was simply the product of his years of military discipline. Whatever the case, the Gurkha's expression softened. He took a step toward Kismet, then knelt beside the shattered form of Singh. When he stood, he held the fallen man's *kukri*.

Gripping the back edge of the broad blade between his thumb and forefinger, he extended the hilt toward Kismet. "When we lay him to rest, I'll want this for his widow. Until then…"

Kismet accepted the knife, acutely aware of the honor Higgins was paying him. He held the blade out, contemplating its balance and the visible keenness of its edge. He then did something that flew in the face of his training. Bringing himself to attention, he saluted the sergeant.

Higgins stiffened respectfully and returned the salute, holding it until Kismet lowered his hand.

"Sergeant, I promise you that we'll give it to her together."

You and I will eventually meet again…

And that's the day I'll cut your heart out, you sick bastard.

But something else Hauser had said gnawed at him.

It was a deeper mystery that he would have to solve before exacting his revenge, a conundrum that would supply impetus to his resolve to survive.

Both Samir and Hauser had known that it would be he, Nick Kismet, coming to supervise the defection. Both men had believed that Kismet would have a particular interest in the ancient—perhaps even holy—treasure unearthed in the ruins of Babylon. But Hauser had added one more dimension to the enigma.

Kismet, if I killed you, your mother would have my head.

Nick Kismet had never known his mother. The woman that had borne him into the world had vanished forever from his life mere moments after completing her labor. No memory or trace of her had remained to prove she ever existed, save for a healthy male child of indeterminate heritage, and a single word, written in the blood of her womb, in a language nearly forgotten; a word that translated alternately as luck, destiny and fate.

A word that had become his name.

ABOUT THE AUTHOR

SEAN ELLIS is the author of several novels. He is a veteran of Operation Enduring Freedom, and has a Bachelor of Science degree in Natural Resources Policy from Oregon State University. He lives with his wife and two sons in Arizona, where he divides his time between writing, adventure sports, and trying to figure out how to save the world.

Visit him online at www.seanellisthrillers.webs.com.